# THE
# VAMPIRE
# SEDUCTION HANDBOOK

# THE
# VAMPIRE
## SEDUCTION HANDBOOK
### A Guide to the Ultimate Romantic Adventure

## Luc Richard Ballion

#### with Scott Bowen

##### Illustrations by Liza Corbett

Skyhorse Publishing

Skyhorse Publishing books may be purchased in bulk at special discounts for sales promotion, corporate gifts, fund raising, or educational purposes. Special editions can also be created to specifications. For details, contact Special Sales Department, Skyhorse Publishing, 555 Eighth Avenue, Suite 903, New York, NY 10018 or info@skyhorsepublishing.com.

www.skyhorsepublishing.com

10 9 8 7 6 5 4 3 2 1

Library of Congress Cataloging-in-Publication Data

Ballion, Luc Richard.
 The vampire seduction handbook : a guide to the ultimate romantic adventure / Luc Richard Ballion, with Scott Bowen.
     p. cm.
  ISBN 978-1-60239-746-0
 1. Vampires--Humor. 2. Love--Humor. 3. Sex--Humor. 4. Seduction--Humor. I. Bowen, Scott. II. Title.
  PN6231.V27B36 2009
  818'.607--dc22
                        2009020407

Printed in China

For all those who have given me shelter and sustenance. And for Violet.

—LRB

My thanks to those family members who introduced me to vampires. And thanks to LRB, a born storyteller, and to Ann T., a great editor.

—SB

# Contents

# THE
# VAMPIRE
## SEDUCTION HANDBOOK

# Introduction

I have not lived long as a vampire, just two hundred some years. Older, venerable vampires would regard me as not much more than a stripling. I did, however, become a vampire just at the moment when this country actually became a country, and I have lived here ever since. In that time, I have met and loved numerous human women, mostly American women—the most exciting kind. And, I did, indeed, drink their blood. That's what we vampires do.

Of course, your first question is: Did I ever kill any of them? No, I did not, first and foremost because that just complicates things for the vampire, given that our greatest protection is the camouflage of legend. I saw no point in ever drawing any attention to myself or kind by leaving a trail of exsanguinated barmaids, seamstresses, dancers, artists, heiresses, secretaries, and prominent wives. But men and other vampires I have indeed killed—because they came looking for violent trouble and found it with me.

I am a vampire forged in war—the first one against the British—and I've no love of violence, but I wield it as rightly as the sword I took from the damned Hessian who bit me those years ago, and then poured his own dank, Teutonic blood into my mouth. I'm much more interested in the pleasures I have known, and will continue to know, from those *fanciulla gentile* who have willingly and lustfully let me drink their blood. They brought me life and pleasure, and in their desire for me they spoke no word of my existence, although I made sure they were aware of my dangerous fury should they ever point out my place of concealment. You have to look out for yourself, you know.

For vampires, the consumption of blood *is* sexual and it is endlessly pleasurable and complicated, because blood is life for us and can keep us alive for many, many years. Vampires do enjoy the physicality of intercourse and other sexual practices as you know them, but these are corollaries to the main action: drinking blood directly from you. The sensation of your blood filling our bellies and soaking our muscles brings to every cell in our bodies an orgasmic pleasure of life itself.

Some people will exclaim that sex with vampires is tantamount to necrophilia. This is uninformed narrow-mindedness. Vampires are "alive" in the same sense that all other animals are alive—we eat, breathe, move about, act upon our instincts and thoughts, and can suffer a true death. We simply fall in a different place on the evolutionary scale, having converted to an older physiology through a process that took us much closer to real death than any human could endure (any human who has not been given vampire blood).

I drink your blood to survive, and if I admire you, need you, have a deep, profound liking for you, or, indeed, love you, then I might give you *my* blood and transform you into a vampire. That is the ultimate act of the vampire in a relationship with a woman. I have in my time, for highly selective reasons, converted just two women (and also a few men, needed as vampire warriors). Every species must propagate itself. But the vampire must do so with utmost, history-making care, as if selecting a king or general, or mate.

In most of my romances, I enjoyed the company of a daring, inquisitive woman for weeks, months, sometimes years, and lived off her bright red bounty. You might think that on the whole, such relationships are unbalanced—my kind and I appear to take from you while frequently giving little in return, because we can't convert all you humans willy-nilly. But we vampires do offer a great deal: companionship, love, sex, friendship, and the potential for a very exciting romance. We can also protect you, and keep you safe, in both times of peace and times of danger. The vampire is something of a righteous outlaw—a being that does not ascribe to human law, but does right by his friends and keeps safe the woman he loves. Imagine being a single woman knowing that a beneficent, if hungry, vampire is looking out for you? Your lawyer/doctor/hockey player/

senator boyfriend can't match a vampire's ability to completely neutralize any threat to you.

But there is little of the "unconditional" between a vampire and his woman lover. But among you humans, love and sex and fun continually hinge upon the correct combination of the right conditions. Surely, you say, "I'd do anything for so-and-so," or, "I'd risk my life for him." Vampires do the same, you will find. But ask yourself, "Why would I do such things in the first place?" The answer is obvious: because you *need* that person for whom you extend yourself, and that need is in itself a condition. There is no "unconditional" in this world, yours or mine. Nature didn't make us that way.

We vampires need you, dear humans, much more than you could ever need us. Because of that, we are much more careful about you than you think. In general, we must maintain the veil of myth. We cannot stride the full public stage; we are always in the wings or under the boards, out of the lights. We can never cause so much trouble in such a widespread way that vampire eradication becomes as common a practice as gassing stray dogs. And believe me, in this modern, Western world, so lacking in superstition or worry of preternatural evil, were you mortals to comprehend the fact that we do exist, a war on us "creatures of the night" would begin quite quickly. In other words, killing you or converting you in numbers is a highly dangerous and forbidden practice. Your trust-through-lust is imperative, dear ladies.

And we so hotly desire you, we vampires who never forgot the kind of men we were before our conversion —men who were infused, pure and simple, with desire for women. That is where sex can come in. Blood is so utterly integral to great sex—good circulation, flushed skin, engorged flesh—that it would seem perfectly natural in the intercourse between vampire man and human woman for a little blood to be drawn and drunk as well, now wouldn't it?

It could be the sensuous adventure you've been waiting for.

# 1

# The Vampire Lover

I cannot state that there is a "type" of woman who seeks a vampire lover. In my experience, I never thought I could categorize those I encountered who, once having met me, knowingly and wantingly sought my return. But return I did to women of all walks of life who left a side door or window unlocked, or who met me in a field or woods, under black night clouds or in moonlight.

There is, however, a kind of vampire who evolves into a sort of blood-drinking gallant—one not entirely a killer, but, in essence, one who cultivates an erotic union with a woman for the sake of deriving that life-giving substance. He does so for obvious reasons of survival, but also out of his intensely favoring her individually, because she reminds him of someone he once loved, or wished he had loved; or she appears to him to be one of many ideals of womanly beauty that he cannot refuse, that beauty being interior and exterior, of all shapes and colors.

Given that the vampire needs only to dispense his (or her) blood to any victim to recreate his kind, the former human reproductive imperatives are left behind along with typical human mortality. But the pleasures of the flesh—for blood is a kind of tissue—remain for the vampire.

## What and Who is a Vampire?

What I know of my kind I have learned myself, and from others, and thus know only what they know. There is very little written down about our deepest evolutionary origins, but we did not spring from southeastern Europe only: The vampire evolved globally, alongside *Homo sapiens.* More specifically, a virus resulting from gene mutations occurred far back in human history, and this led to a separate form of humanity, that being which is nonhuman and, as you say, "undead," a great misnomer. This happened for inexplicable reasons, other than to say that it happened for the same reason any other mutation occurs, because DNA is not perfect. No one is aware of actual evidence of a divine or supernatural cause, but the human and vampire mythologies that envelop my kind have created enough of an impression that we are supernatural. Many of us, including myself, are willing to go along with those interpretations when suitable; that is, when religion or superstition effectively distracts the minds of human pursuers, or strikes fear in their hearts. Of course, if you look back across old vampire histories, a good deal of religious practice is involved in human resistance to vampirism, but the stakes, thorns, nails, and needles shot through the vampire's heart and head, and the decapitations and dismemberment and immolation of the vampire body do the real work of ridding a community of the fanged marauder.

So the vampire is a formerly human creature that survives on blood and oxygen, and takes every conceivable form seen in humanity, and then some. I have heard tell of vampiric pirate ships, created by a single vampire captain who converted ruffians, thieves, murderers, and a few giants into a vampire crew that sought bounty on the high seas. Vampires famously trail armies, feasting on the wounded in the aftermath of battle, as happened to me at Brandywine, and have at times converted badly-wounded men out of sheer devilry of making monsters, and sometimes out of the decision to create a servant who as a mortally wounded soldier begged not to be left to die. And, yes, there have been entire brothels of vampires.

We aren't shape-shifters, however. Try as I might, I cannot turn into a wolf, snake, butterfly, or bat, as some superstitions would have it. Mist? Nay, not even methane—the blood diet does not cause flatulence (not a bad adaptation for a predator, eh?). We cannot take the form of a ball of light, as said of the *lougarou* of Haiti. We cannot fly, except on airplanes, although I do recall one fellow who enjoyed hang gliding from his mountain lair to the valley below. There is no parallel universe or satanic dimension into which we venture, back and forth. I am of and bound to this Earth, and so are you.

We do, however, possess great physical strength, owing to our vampire physiology. Our sense of smell is on par with a hound's. We have some thermal capabilities, and can sense body heat—yours. Our eyesight adapts to night, and we see very well in the dark. The full rays of the sun, the combined gamma, ultra-violet, and infrared rays, burn us deeply, because of bodily changes during the transformation from human to vampire. We can function during daylight hours, surely, and we can also cover ourselves for a brief time in the sun, if absolutely necessary. But the sun will kill us; blister us, burn us, and turn us to ash.

There are vampires who, because of the vagaries of the virus, have their own aberrant physiology and ghoulish countenance, or in great age take on fearsome, wizard-like aspects. You could, unfortunately, find yourself attacked by a vampire that does not look like any mortal of this Earth, even though he or she is formerly human.

Of course, that's hardly what you want. You're looking for the leading-man type, no? A befanged George Clooney? Or a young swain, an Orlando Bloom or Omar Epps? Perhaps a musician, a rock star, a blood-sipping Devendra Banhart? Or, as in my day, a decorated soldier?

They exist. They're around. I suppose I could be one myself, the good, nocturnal boyfriend. And given that I write this while looking out the window at the lights of the capital city of this country, we are directly in your midst, ladies.

## Vampire Masculinity—An Introduction

Surely, you've read some vampire stories, be they my favorites—the first generation of Western vampire literature from the 1800s—or more recent. And there are all the movies and television shows, oh so many *bad* movies and television shows. You've absorbed these fictional accounts of vampire masculinity, and they are of great variety and seeming inconsistency.

A male vampire retains a strong sense of his human manliness and sexuality. What changes him is his realization that as a vampire he can do virtually anything and anyone he wants, as human imperatives and limits no longer apply. The necessities of seeking, obtaining, enjoying, and living on blood are what shape vampire behavior.

But the male vampire can hotly desire both female vampires and female humans. Relations with female vampires revolve around finding and managing significant sources of nutrition;

that is, finding and staking out human-rich territory that can be shared as a couple. But female vampires can survive on their own as well as any male, and need not submit to any amorous entreaties from another vampire. Male and female vampires enjoy sex in the same manner as humans, but this is triggered by feeding, and is a pleasure of feeding together.  One vampire might pursue another with a sexual intent, but the act necessitates feeding, although it can also involve the vampires drinking each other's blood.

Vampires feel the same emotions as humans, and we succumb to them as readily, and often more thoroughly. But we contain them better. Thus, while we might appear to be almost mechanical and cold, we seem so because of our intense focus on survival. The passion in our breast stirs us as hotly as it stirs you, and given our existence, we can indulge our feelings much more thoroughly than humans.

The male vampire can come across as a soldiery type or an adventurer; a gentleman or dandy; a poet; the strong, silent type; or brash, mercurial, and unpredictable. In other words, every characteristic a man can have, a vampire can have. It all depends on his experience both as a human and as a vampire, and his situation as a vampire. But overriding all is the male vampire's sense of mission: to feed, survive, and remain an enigma to the human world at large.

Heterosexuality among vampires is as strong as it is for humans. Why, a large part of European gypsy vampire lore, if a bit excitable, centers around highly sexual vampires of both genders: male vampires whose intense sex drive enables them to escape the grave (after burial of the mistakenly "dead" person) and impels them to return to and ravish wives and girlfriends; and female vampires who appear entirely human, but whose sexual appetites take their husbands to the brink of complete exhaustion.

A vampire, of course, cannot relate to you, the human woman, in the same habitual ways that a human man can. He cannot have dinner with you, not in a restaurant. His hours are usually limited to darkness. He is often not marriage minded, alas, though some are. He will not always be inclined to join your social circle, for obvious reasons. You might like to swing dance, ride polo ponies, or play video games, and enjoy the social scene attendant to each. But your vampire will not feel any inclination to participate or meet your teammates, as socializing in the human world is both impossible and off-limits.

On other matters, however, a vampire lover can be completely solicitous. He will meet you when least expected to make sure you get home safe. He will take you places you wish to go, because travel is a particular love of vampires, as a change of location is often a good thing. Most material possessions are within his grasp, as he might steal when it suits him, and he often likes to adorn his lover with clothes and jewels that favor her. He is a restraining order made flesh, scourge of ex-boyfriends or ex-husbands who won't leave you alone. In times of real danger he will watch over you even if you don't know he's there. The male vampire can be utterly faithful in his heart; he will love you only if he says he does. But he cannot control his necessity for sustenance, and will drink blood from other women as from men. If he lies down with another woman, he will do so for sustenance, not love.

Why do we sleep with you, our human lover? Because you remind us of our lives as men, and of the beautiful thing we vampires are no longer—a human with limited time. You have a softness, sweetness, and sexual mortality that make every kiss and every quake shockingly beautiful. You are not going to be this way

Soon after I was turned into a vampire in 1777, I encountered numerous other young fellows lurking at the edges of society, in the dark, who had also suffered the same fate during the War for Independence. As we were of the same former social ilk, in a nation of humans who were united as a country by a hatred of taxation and a strong sense of liberty, we smartly and rightly formed a coven in Philadelphia, as we thought we should stay where the action was (the city was the capital at the time). Our youth and handsomeness made us something of a company of would-be swains, if we were only human, but we saw no point in limiting ourselves, and so we pursued the ladies of Philadelphia, from the Main Line to the river wharfs. Eventually, some of these women joined our coven. We now number some sixty members.

forever; your body will not be this way forever. But for a short time or a long time, your body and soul can be this way with a different kind of man who can let you act upon your deepest, wildest desires, and even allow you to step entirely out of your societal and familial role to become, sexually, a woman you never knew.

Therein is the gist of our connection: When you are with your vampire, you are a woman who loves a vampire, and are thus unlike any other sort of woman you could be in your world. When I am with you, I am more vampire than I've ever been, because I am the whole of vampirism that you know. You contain my living sustenance. I give you the chance to connect with a primordial sexuality hidden in every woman that is only rarely attained in a sex life dependent upon other humans, all of you enclosed in your roles. The vampire has only a simple role within humanity: to feed, to protect, to love, and to convert those who should be vampires.

## Does a Vampire Lover Have to Drink Your Blood?

Amid the hundreds of cinematic and television dramas about vampires, there have been recent programs that have taken a novel approach to the issue of drinking blood, in particular, the use of artificial-blood beverages and the practice of human-blood abstinence. Certainly, these ideas have crossed the minds of many

# The Blood State

**Another term for living as a vampire Is living "the blood state," i.e.,** surviving on blood alone. And you should know that vampires follow a basic set of rules called "The Factors of Blood," which greatly affect how your vampire romance and relationship can and will proceed. In a sense, these are myth-busting practices, because we have had to learn the hard way that monstrous or murderous behavior only gets us into trouble and makes enjoying our lives and loves all the more difficult.

**Take just the blood you need:** Blood, like any natural resource, exists in limited quantities at any one time. Every vampire knows each victim can surrender only so much blood without danger.

**Do not kill in the act of feeding:** You don't kill the golden goose—you manage it. Dead people produce no more blood, and drinking up humans and leaving their bodies around like piles of empty beer bottles will just make the Feds suspicious.

**Subdue human memory:** Being fed upon must be so dazzling, frightening, hypnotic, or overpowering that the person remembers the merest details only, and surely cannot bring her- or himself to believe an actual vampire visited them.

**Convert a victim under extreme necessity only:** Those vampires organized into covens are well aware that a steady population of vampires, both locally and globally, is a way to ensure survival overall. There are plenty of lone vampires converting numerous victims, with lots of unpleasant results. But those of us who take seriously our continued survival and secrecy make careful selections about which humans we purposefully bring into the blood state. That's not to say we don't do so out of love.

a vampire in the modern age, and anything that helps stabilize vampire-to-human relationships is a good thing. But a vampire truly does have a very difficult time *not doing* what vampires do, and there will always be those blood drinkers who scoff at the idea of avoiding human blood for the sake of integrating ourselves a bit more into human society.

If a vampire really likes you, he is most certainly going to drink your blood. By the same token, he's not going to drain you completely. He's no fool (see Factors of Blood). Tasting your blood does not turn a vampire into a raving sex maniac. He can easily drink your blood, and leave it with a smile. Or, drink your blood while you are both doing your best to maintain the swan position. It all depends on the context of his interaction with you.

**A Cleansing Ritual** Viruses and bacteria that a vampire takes in from drinking human blood rarely manifest themselves because they do not find a workable host. These microbes soon perish in the vampire's system, and thus cannot be transmitted through the bite itself, or the vampire's saliva. But if a vampire has just fed on a human infected with a contagion, and soon feeds on you, blood cells from the infected victim could still be in the vampire's mouth, and be transferred to you. So a proper vampire who feeds before visiting you will go through a cleansing ritual before he arrives to attend to you, or can do so in your premises. Set out a bowl of very warm water, a washcloth, natural soap, good toothpaste, a toothbrush, a nail brush, a pitcher of cool water, a small bottle of vodka or straight grain alcohol, and a cup. The vodka and water mix is in lieu of mouthwash, because the strong chemical mint or other flavor can throw off the taste of your blood, but the alcohol in the vodka (or grain alcohol) acts as an oral sterilizing agent. As a way of initiating contact, you might help him wash his hands, face, and neck, and rub in a little moisturizer. Some vampires find the cleaning ritual relaxing while at the same time heightening their anticipation of you.

If a vampire uses a dagger or stiletto, such as I do, he will include this in the cleaning ritual. All he will need for this is a candle flame or the vodka, or both. Keeping the dagger sharp is something he will do on his own.

Many vampires, myself included, use stilettos and feeding flutes with willing partners. My fangs are perfectly fine, but I find that with a stiletto I am able to make a perfectly placed and sized puncture that goes just deep enough, and that of course does not leave a recognizable bite mark, something that can be crucial to a vampire's camouflage. My girlfriend will show just a small nick on her skin at one of several most accessible feeding points—the carotid artery; the brachial, radial, and ulnar arteries in the arm; and the femoral, posterior tibial, and dorsalis pedis arteries in the leg—and this can be easily ascribed to a simple accident. The vampire lover also keeps in mind his woman's fashion sense: If her wardrobe shows off her arms and neck, shoulders and breasts, he's a fool to leave a bite mark anywhere.

Now, take note of what I say here: You cannot, as a human, sustain regular feedings. You'll be anemic by the weekend. Blood is mostly water, and while water is crucial, so is protein, and to get enough of that, a vampire, especially a vigorous and healthy one, needs a lot of blood on any given night, about three English pints, at a minimum. A vampire, much like a snake or crocodile, can go for long periods without feeding, but that is dangerous and no vampire does so willingly. So while you will be the one he bites in love, you are not the only one he loves to bite.

In times of vampiric famine, i.e., when no people are about, or when there is no chance to feed on people, a vampire can live off mammals: cows, horses, sheep, rats, as well as larger birds. In truly dire times, reptiles can be added to that list. European vampire folklore is full of instances of vampires preying upon livestock, and there are numerous, defunct rituals that herders and farmers conduct with livestock to ward off vampires. A vampire, however, might choose to feed on livestock even if humans are available, because of quantity, given that a full-grown Angus cow contains four to five gallons of blood and can give up a good amount to a vampire who wants to fill his belly so that he can sip daintily from his woman's neck and cause her no measurable blood loss.

And, indeed, you could extract from a devoted vampire the promise that he will feed from livestock only when he drinks blood other than yours, but that is a promise made of love or extreme admiration of a woman. It does happen. I did so just twice, but did so willingly, and yet, in the end, I did not convert either woman into the blood state. However, I did drink their blood, too, because a vampire must have *some* human blood, as our sheer state of being demands it, and our throats, our tongues, our noses, and our guts demand that warm, chocolatey-rusty, salty-sweet liquor. All the better it comes from a woman we adore.

# 2

# The Woman-Vampire Connection

Before I continue on about the male vampire-to-woman relationship, allow me to point out that history is rife with female vampires of all sorts, and that they pursue victims of both sexes with as much alacrity as I would pursue them myself. Two of the great works of vampire literature of the 1800s, Samuel Taylor Coleridge's poem *Christabel* and Sheridan Le Fanu's novella *Carmilla,* both feature female vampires. And while these are fictionalized accounts, they are accurate in their depiction of the emotional register of the human-vampire attraction.

But you don't as often see human men desire a female vampire as women desire the male vampire. Why is this?

I think it has to do with masculine issues of submission. Men are just not as willingly and curiously submissive as most women, on the whole, and cannot so easily put themselves in a relationship with a vampire because it is too unbalanced—there is too much the vampire controls. Men are in a constant struggle for control of their professional and personal lives because that's just the way human men turn out, and how I remember it well (I joined Washington's army to take control of my very destiny as a would-be American, but this was a good turn of mind).

Thus, most men miss out on the thrills of submission that women have long enjoyed along with their inherent ability to take sexual charge of men. Submission is not a total surrender of control nor is it a permanent surrender of power. It is momentary, although it can be total in that one moment. It can be structured and specific, and have limits, but remain a constant factor for a woman and her vampire lover.

## Why Women Fall for Vampires

I was a married man when I nearly died at the Battle of Brandywine, so I well know the human feeling of wanting to give oneself to someone. Vampires do not often experience the same feelings for humans. When they do, however, they tend to be a bit obsessive about it, but that's the nature of this beast.

In my experience over these 233 years, not counting my twenty-six human years, I have decided there are six main reasons why women seek us: intensity of feeling, protection, the attraction of our power, the adventure of the affair, the sex, and the effect on identity.

The first factor, intensity of feeling, derives from what has often been described as a vampire's ability to hypnotize humans. We can do so, of sorts. We have a kind of animal magnetism, like what you might experience when you look into the face of a wolf (having done so at a zoo myself). That predatory gaze combined with our arresting physical presence creates a very heady, emotional atmosphere between our desired female and us. Vampires also tend to be insistent and very direct, and thus overwhelm human manners, leaving a woman without much room to maneuver. The sum of the effect for the woman is to feel that she is the object of wild desire, which imbues both feelings of excitement and loss of control.

Also, many vampires whisper or sing with a sibilant voice to humans as they stalk them, lulling them or getting inside their heads, much like the sirens did to Odysseus. A vampire lover frequently does the same to his woman as a form of seduction. We also purposefully pique human curiosity—we play tricks by making odd sounds in the dark, or play games by moving your personal items, forcing you to go looking for them, making you walk right to us. This is a kind of bloodletting foreplay for us. For you, it only heightens the affect of connective sensual intensity that draws a woman to us.

A second reason women fall for a vampire lover is his ability to protect her. As I said earlier, a vampire smitten or in love with a woman will clear away all threats to her, and will usually make this known to her at the beginning of their affair. Aside from what danger he himself might present, a woman in the thrall of vampire love knows she has little to fear from any human enemies—as long as her fellow tofu munchers have no idea what she's up to. But I'll speak on the subject of secrecy later.

The power of a vampire is another major attraction, and when I say "power," I mean a vampire's ability to obtain and deliver various things. Human objects of desire— a diamond or emerald ring, a rare book or kitten—do not hold the same sway over vampires, and a vampire lover will give such things gladly to his human lover if he knows they will make her happy. Above all, a cunning vampire is a master thief. Vampires can also find people—they have access to an extensive network of vampire intelligence, and can locate other humans. I have perhaps a dozen times found long-lost family members and friends of my woman lovers, as I knew this would bring no end of happiness and relief, and favors.

For many women, the sheer wildness and adventure of loving a vampire is what drives them to the places and times where they might meet one. These women tend to be the most game and vibrant of all, but they are also those most steeped in human vampire media, and expect a frolic akin to something they enjoyed while playing masquerade. *C'est le sang.* They instead find themselves in

Back in the early 1960s I regularly visited a woman in a suburb of Dallas, Texas. I developed a sudden interest in mountain climbing, so I said to her, "Let's go climb Mount Rainier." After four days' travel, and snacking on six unwitting victims across the west, we set off just after sunset into the foothills of Ranier, backpacks, headlamps, and ropes in tow. Around ten o'clock the following night, I fed upon her heavily—having encountered no other climbers at night on that dangerous crag—and we cavorted happily on an upper slope. Now that was an adventurous woman. I even offered to convert her, but she declined, having been raised to a premier level of Texan femininity she did not want to relinquish.

a situation that taxes them to almost no end, and only a certain type—a true sexual adventurer with no unbreakable attachments—manages to keep up.

Also, some people are aroused by fear. Fear is always a bit arousing—it is central to the life of the vampire, which is a life of high physiological arousal, a nearly animal state. Some women seek a relationship with a vampire to fulfill a fear fantasy. Others want to experience the feeling of being intimate with an extremely dangerous entity. Some have a religious need to confront what they perceive as demonic. Some just want to feel their bodies shake. Surely legions of women's studies PhDs abhor the idea that some women get off on fear, but I have seen it myself, and I am not brutish for the sake of being brutish.

Ah yes, then. The sex. A properly-fed male vampire can get it up and keep it up for some time, and enjoys merrily the thrash of sex as it sloshes the blood meal, which causes more rapid absorption, heating him up and maximizing his circulation, and thus, in turn, heightening his libido and pleasure. It's nearly a perfect system, no? A certain amount of physical vigor is necessary for a male vampire to reach orgasm, usually quite a bit more than the usual human male. In other words, my dear ladies, you're going to get jiggled and jostled and tossed and banged quite thoroughly as your vampire reaches his climax. Invariably, a vampire will feed on you during sex, which might make you a bit dizzy, heightening your own pleasure as it lowers your inhibition. He would also be aided greatly by having a good quantity of blood already in him, which would necessitate a couple of feedings before he arrives at your chamber door. As mentioned earlier, you're going to have to come to an agreement about that, and the caring and fastidious vampire will begin the night with a proper cleansing ritual.

Lastly, I have found that women seek a vampire lover for whatever transformational effect he might have on their lives. This sounds a bit clichéd, I know, much like the reason women give for having affairs with human men. But a woman with any sense knows a vampire will alter her in myriad ways, and the woman who knowingly seeks a vampire is seeking something more transformational than a fling. Who you are after several months of vampire romance will be quite different from the person who sought a vampire in the first place. Your life, habits, and view of the world will have been altered greatly. You will probably have a more keen view of your friends and fellow human beings, though that's not to say that a vampire will rob you of any sensitivity and compassion. But to be involved with someone tantamount to a criminal, and whose night-by-night survival hinges on a high level of precaution, is to understand and even participate in a life

## A Note About the Word "Victim"

In a post politically correct world, people want to repudiate or "reclaim" that word, for a variety of reasons. I do not pity those humans on whom I feed *because* I feed on them. However, they have fallen prey to me, no?

I'm not sure how else to refer to them. Other vampires are less charitable, referring to their human prey as "the blood," "meat," "birds," "buds," and "punks."

So if "victim" carries any stigma, that stigma (no pun intended there) should be a term that acts as a description of the fact that the person has been physically reduced, and also was possibly in some danger. It is not meant to suggest some kind of incompetence or culpability, or something wrong with the person.

in which you have real enemies, both human and possibly vampire. You will have to come to terms with the schedules, occasional banality, artificial calmness, and categorization of human existence that are challenged by the vampire and your desire for a vampire.

## Lesbian Vampires

Just as there are male vampires who desire females, there are female vampires who want the same, and those human women who desire a female vampire. A woman vampire who makes use of certain sexual implements can physically possess the form of both male and female, bite your neck, and give you a maximum vamp-sexual experience, should you wish that. So if you are a woman who prefers women, then close your eyes and imagine your perfect female archetype transformed into a vampire with belted-in strap-on, and you've got yourself one hell of a Fourth of July coming to you, don't you?

That said, you can find any sexual permutation you want in the vampire world. No one makes much of a fuss about who's with whom as long as the blood flows healthfully and no one gets killed. Dead humans—er, the *wrong* dead humans—draw attention of police and families. Dead vampires draw the attention of vengeful covenmates.

Homophobia as it is known and practiced in the human world is laughably naive in the vampire world. I pay scant attention to whom my fellow vampires romance, as long as their business does not detrimentally affect mine; that is, if somebody gets in the way of my proper nutrition or puts designs on the woman I desire.

## The Bond of Blood

Note above, where I say "as long as the blood flows *healthfully . . .*" That particular adverb applies both ways: The human prey gives up enough blood without going into a coma or dying, or being wrung out for days, and the vampire gets enough nutrition to validate the effort.

But blood between lovers becomes much more a substance of shared desire. For the vampire, drinking his lover's blood becomes wholly necessary to his enjoyment of her. In other words, after time, he will not be able to touch you or look at you without soon tasting your blood, even if it's just a drop. Don't be surprised if a sudden kiss turns into a quick drink. That's honest lust, vampire style.

Do not be disgusted by the presence or appearance of blood during sex. That tends to be a problem with you humans, owing either to taboos about cleanliness, disease, or violence. While you are at your most intimate and physically connected, your lover will deftly draw blood, mostly to drink, but many vampires also enjoy the appearance of blood on their lover's skin. Blood is too precious to waste, but a bit will be drawn and spread on your skin so that the vampire can smell you all the more enjoyably, and lick you pleasurably while you make love.

The scent and taste of your blood will become inexorably tied to your vampire's desire for you. This is sometimes referred to as the "bond of blood," in which your blood comes to embody for the vampire everything about you: your physical, emotional, and sexual nourishment; your reciprocal feelings; and your love for him. Eventually, you will develop a wild excitement, even pleasure to orgasm, at the thought of his feeding from your neck or wrist.

## Physical Attractions and Demands

Vampires can be as vain or empathetic as humans about a potential partner. They can pursue a human lover solely on the basis of looks, be those looks waifish, voluptuous, or depraved. You might simply have a very healthful appearance, one that hints at sweet blood underneath, and your vampire's attraction grows from there. A vampire might find that you have an adventurous physique—combination of body, mind, and ability—and think you could possibly be someone who might be aroused by and capable of enduring the human-vampire bond.

You might also remind a vampire of a lost love, someone he left behind in the mortal world after entering the blood state. The vampire world is full of both male and female vampires bereft of

love because a human spouse or companion refused to love them
once they became vampires, owing to a lack of open-mindedness
and courage; in many of these cases, the vampire refrained from
converting the human-former partner. While, in other situations,
a vampire did convert a wife or husband, only to lose that person
after he or she became a vampire. So these kinds of attractions can

be the most powerful kind. A long future is the vampire's to inhabit if he (or she) is most careful about the present. But the human past that lingers in a vampire's memory can haunt him like a bad dream, and my kind, myself included, occasionally lunge at the chance to mend or reconnect virtually to some part of that past.

What will physically attract you to a vampire? That will depend on your tastes and needs, your personal history, and your degree of sexual freedom. Say you meet a vampire and are stunned by the way he dresses, his natural fox-fire eyes, and his ability to tango—something he learned in Buenos Aires in 1895. Maybe he also resembles a respected, or conflicted, male figure (dad? uncle? a professor?) and has a sheer physical presence—his "countenance and figure" as they said in my day—that you cannot ignore. Your degree of sexual freedom, however, is a bit trickier.

When I was a young human man, I married for love, but I also married out of desire for a steady woman in my life. I had, I thought, tired of the chase. I liked having her lie down beside me at night, and I liked awakening next to her in the dawn. Humans tend to prefer that kind of consistency, and with good reason. You will have something of the same with a vampire lover, but you will not always know when or if he will arrive, or when you will meet him next. Can you maintain a romantic connection with a human man at the same time you also have a vampire boyfriend? Or, could you break entirely from intercourse with human men, and delve entirely into a world of vampire sex and love, strange as it is?

In other words, what are the margins of your sexual behavior, and how far can you push them? When your vampire man shows up with two female vampire friends in tow, what do you say—"We didn't talk about this" or "Give me the blonde one"?

That's an exaggerated example. But it leads us to the next item: the physical demands of being the vampire's girlfriend. You're going to stay up late *a lot.* You're going to contort yourself on occasion, or possibly hang from the ceiling by your ankles. You will, as numerous popular songs declare, rock 'n' roll all night long, if you don't pass out. (I can remember when the expression "rock 'n' roll" made reference to something other than an actual musical form.)

Therefore, you will have to be in reasonably good physical condition, meaning that you have to possess a certain quantity of both force and stamina, which varies from person to person. I knew a flapper at the Green Mill club in Chicago who weighed ninety pounds in her scant clothes, and could drink champagne and dance the Charleston all night after I took a half pint from her. I knew a burlesque dancer in New Orleans who might have tipped the scales at 190, and she actually exhausted me a few times; she could also twirl her tassels in opposite directions while pinning me in the vise

I once had a friend, a huge Turk, who fell victim to a vampire during a smallpox outbreak in 1820 in Charleston, South Carolina, during which he also was struck partly blind. He saved my life (I was being pursued by the most relentless gang of vampire killers I ever knew before World War II), and in return, I helped him leave his haunt, a horrid coastal swamp, where he hid his pox-ravaged form, and I took him to a city where he could join a coven as a guard. Along the way, I found a woman lover, who eventually said she would do anything for me. I took her to my Turk friend and told her to let him feed from her, as he had not known the taste of human blood nor the scent and touch of a woman in many years. She did so. He did not ravage her, but fed from her wrist with a most delicate politeness, and then would have cried, if a Turk would permit himself that. She was shocked by his appearance, but she had an emotional and physical fortitude that stood her well. She died old and rich.

of her thighs. But both of these women had one thing in common: They could dance for hours on end, something that delights me, and which is also something that, done often enough, gives you an endurance that will do you well when you are off your feet.

You will have to perform a few physical feats, such as traveling by foot at night over rough terrain, although your vampire can carry you, if you wish: Sexist I'm not; cordial, yes. Your vampire might enjoy the chase around the house, or want to tie you up, or spank you. If you bruise easily, you will be bruised.

You must also have a strong stomach, not because you will be asked to drink blood, but you will have to have the nerve to witness or engage in those things that vampires like to do, which can sometimes be strange, or messy, or frightening. For example, I knew a very refined vampire who greatly enjoyed horse blood, but the horses, which rarely take happily to a vampire's clutch, scared his girlfriend so much he eventually had to go to the stables alone. In another instance, a former confectioner who had become a vampire tried to show his girlfriend, who was a chef, how to make blood candies and jellies, but having been raised in England and repulsed by traditional blood puddings, she just couldn't bring herself to do it. Another vampire of my acquaintance actually liked to dress up like Batman, with his girlfriend as Robin, and go creeping about a large eastern city, pouncing upon petty criminals and thugs to administer what some call a "tune-up." But the woman did not share his enjoyment of what might otherwise be viewed as vigilantism.

# The Risks of Conversion and Death

The Hessian vampire who drained me and then made me drink his blood on that night-dark battlefield did so to press me into his jaeger coven, in much the same way human Hessians roamed the Westphalia countryside, waylaying and pressing into service poor fellows—students, tradesmen, wanderers—so unlucky as to have crossed paths with those bluecoated mercenaries. The world is not just.

The same could happen to you, in any number of ways, if you become involved with a vampire. He himself might decide that you deserve the immortality of the blood state, and force it upon you the way it might have been forced upon him; a decent fellow won't do this, but one who is a bit more deterministic might make the decision for you. Vampires, being vampires, find their existence a good deal more impressive than being human.

Or, you might find yourself highly desirous of becoming a vampire, and this is something that you will have to examine about yourself before you embark upon your pursuit of this romance. You might see its advantages, and, as I have seen in some women, become obsessed with beginning an entirely new life, casting away every mistake or fault of your human history (see chapter 8 for a more thorough discussion of your interest in conversion). Be careful what you think you should wish for, because if you beg long and strong enough, you might convince your fanged fellow to put his blood-seeping wrist to your mouth.

Once you do become a vampire, however, you cannot expect your lover to act and do the same. After all, you are now a powerful creature capable of defending yourself. But he will certainly continue to desire and love you. He might also, at the beginning, school you as to your new ways of existence. You might stay together as vampires for an eternity, in a permanent marriage. This is something that most often appeals to those humans, both female and male, who fear more than physical aging itself the loss of love due to the eventual loss of life. More about this later.

Additionally, while involved with a vampire, you will be at risk of conversion at the hands of a predatory vampire in pursuit of you, your boyfriend, or both of you. Protecting you from other vampires is a much more difficult task for your lover than fighting off troublesome humans. In my experience, I have only rarely allowed other vampires to know the true identity of my human girlfriend, and infrequently mingled with my beloved in vampire social scenes. You might ask your vampire to do the same.

# Necessities of Conversion

To convert a human being into a vampire, a vampire must first drink a good deal of a victim's blood, and then introduce a replacement quantity of his blood back into the victim, either by having the victim drink his blood or by a transfusion, which is faster and better for returning the victim's blood pressure to normal. The blood that the vampire drank is already blending with his blood, and conversion actually starts in the vampire's veins, with the vampire's blood cells converting the blood cells of the victim, reworking the DNA in the nucleus of each blood cell. Once this "activated" blood goes into the victim, it begins to convert the human on a cellular level into a vampire. Quantity is an important issue. You must be reduced to the barest volume of blood you can endure before enough vampire blood can be introduced to change you. A human can imbibe a very small quantity of diluted vampire blood, mixed with water or wine, and not enter conversion, as occurs during a vampire wedding.

As for dying, for love or any other reason, the chance is always in play. I came of age in a time in which a nick of the straight razor could turn lethal, yet all the while I found a full beard unsuitable and took the risk of shaving. There is the chance of infection from a vampire that opens you with his teeth rather than a blade. You could become an unwitting pawn of vampire treachery, killed for the damage your death will cause your vampire man, were he caught in some trouble with his kind—possibly the most dangerous of all the actions your human counterparts will take when they discover the true nature of your nocturnal consort. And what do you think your religiously-fundamentalist father would do if he found out that you lie down with a "demon"? You could be banished from home, locked in a sanatorium, or fall to the knife of an "honor killing," all depending on the degree of your family's anger, fear, and delusion, and how well they keep their mouths shut about your sudden disappearance.

Now, before you read any further, I should ask you, are you a bleeder? Does your fluid tissue tend to not coagulate well, or not at all? Is there any hemophilia in your family? This is usually something that "royalty" only need worry about, as the tendency of royal bloodlines not to branch very far allows expression of such aberrations of the normal human system. But excessive bleeding could affect anyone. Vampires are experts at dealing with this, knowing how to quickly close wounds or apply natural coagulants at the site. Despite that, hemorrhaging can still kill a vampire's beloved if she suffers from such a disorder.

More than likely, you already know if you have this problem. So, what to do if you do bleed dangerously and uncontrollably, and yet have an insatiable attraction to a being such as me? You would be seeking the most rare vampire lover of all, one who can apply his passions without ever tasting a single drop of you. I do not know who he is, as I am afraid he does not exist.

# 3

# Finding Your Vampire

Vampires are reasonably abundant but tend to inhabit cities small and large. Here and there, they make their home in the suburbs and smaller towns, too—the abundance of high-quality blood in so-called "bedroom communities" is too good to pass up, but the social stratification and the everyone-knows-everyone's-business syndrome of a Springfield, Middletown, or Lawyerville are tantamount to a local reconnaissance-and-intelligence service that makes the hunt for blood a tad more tricky than the situation found in densely populated areas.

What if you live in a rural place? There are country vampires, too. But in places of low population density, the care with which they must operate is very great, as they have only so many residents and passersby on whom to feed. They can be easily noticed if they make just one slip, and thus will tend to prey upon passersby much more than actual residents. That said, there are rural situations that I will discuss.

Ninety-nine times out of a hundred, a vampire chooses you. He sees you, he picks you, he pursues you. We *hunt* people. But there have been those women who have, through their own determination and craftiness, managed to close in on an individual vampire and make him reveal himself. This is tantamount to a full-time job. And you also cannot know exactly if a local vampire is male or female until you see him or her in action, that action usually being the swooping-down-upon-you part.

But there are ways to push your luck, and close the gap between you and a blood-drinking suitor.

## Venturing into the Night

Actually spotting and pursuing a vampire of your choosing is quite difficult. While you surely want to find one whom you think is right, you ability to select your vampire exists in inverse proportion to the chances of his selecting you. You might have to endure a few odd encounters before you get close to your ideal of a "nice guy."

But here are a few ways to close the gap. You are voluntarily courting danger doing these things, of course, but what's another night of popcorn and Netflix going to do for your love life?

## The Mark of the Vampire

I'm giving away any number of facts about my kind in writing this book. Much of that is of no consequence. But there are a few things I cannot tell you about in detail, and one of those things is vampire graffiti.

Vampires not known to each other communicate in public through scrawls, drawings, and symbols. These are often small, highly stylized, and disguised within human graffiti or disguised to look just like human graffiti. This writing will appear much as a cross between Arabic and Cyrillic characters. If you look carefully and steadily in various places, you will begin to see them. This graffiti might be carved into wood, drawn with a Sharpie or spray paint, or written by a finger dipped in blood. Sometimes a vampire will make a faint mark—drawn on or carved into the wood—above a doorway, along the eaves of a building, or on a corner joist. This is a mark meant to stake out very immediate territory, to convey a message to other vampires that they are within hunting ground established by a resident vampire and should keep moving. (Poaching is not a welcome activity in my world, although it is tolerated to some degree in places of abundant and healthy humans, for, on a certain level, a resident vampire is a gamekeeper.)

How do you make this information work for you? Take a walk around your town or neighborhood during the day, and try to find such scrawlings and marks. Map them, and at night take a walk in a pattern through the area they demarcate. Tag yourself with a small item of red—a silk scarf, choker, or ribbon in your hair— against otherwise dark clothes. Make several laps. Repeat this over several concurrent nights. You will most certainly be noticed. If nothing happens after the first attempt, stop, and wait, and try again after a few weeks.

Indeed, this sounds like the routine of a certain professional woman. But the habits of making yourself available, on foot, in public, follow certain patterns regardless of intention. You won't be the first woman trying to do this who might be mistaken for someone strutting her wares.

Don't be disappointed if you are left alone after several ventures through a given territory. The vampire who made the marks you found might have already moved on. Or he, or she, might simply be too cautious to glom on to a human female who is obviously trying to make amorous contact, as vampire hunters have often made use of this tactic. A local vampire might also simply have no interest in a human companion, maintaining a view of you as prey only. But you're banking on the odds that the vampire who left these marks is your type.

Knowing to look for these marks, you can use this information to put yourself in circulation in a number of locations.

## Nightclubbing

The first and obvious thing is to look for a place that has sufficient human nightlife. Some vampires will circulate at the edges of this activity, while others have the ability to pass

(mostly) for human within a nocturnal milieu. Disguises wear thin quickly in this day and age, however, and a vampire will take on a human guise or role only briefly, for the sake of a quick accomplishment, be that finding a specific prey, or some other immediate goal.

The locations and reputations of such venues—clubs, bars, regular but private parties, gambling houses, brothels— will not be prominent. They'll be places worth going to, for what is found there, but they will have a certain out-of-the-wayness about them. The managers and patrons of these places will prefer to enjoy themselves under-the-radar, a difficult accomplishment in an age when the media pokes into every corner, however sooty and sticky, sniffing for the hip new thing.

Go to such places at specific times of night, and repeat those times, again tagged with a piece of red in your dress. As you approach this location, always approach from the same starting point and move in the same way. When you leave, walk a circle of the block, or two, stopping at given points, places of easy concealment.

Yes, you are making yourself available at the same time that you seek. You are your own bait. Not much different from the usual human romance, is it?

And what of these "vampire clubs," or vampire cults, or gothy gatherings in general—are these places where a vampire could go, where so many humans indulge their love of the vampiric? It is amusing for us to do so, yes. The blending in part is a hoot (I have a goth *Star Trek* outfit that puts my friends on the floor with laughter). Such social vampire clubs, populated by humans, have often supplied a good deal of nutrition for my kind. Goth girls also provide a particular kind of camouflage, for who would question a young gal straight out of a Camille Rose Garcia painting who says, "My boyfriend is a vampire"? *Of course* her boyfriend is a vampire. Who would find that odd? She shouldn't, however, go telling anyone.

But even in such gatherings of willing and happy prey, the vampire is careful as ever about selecting a human lover, as opposed to simply feeding off a latex-clad gal out for a weekend of fun.

## Parks and Urban "Green Zones"

The footbridge in Forest Park, St. Louis, is an old favorite vampire haunt. There's a famous mark of a vampire at the foot of the bridge, going into the park, but that fellow is long gone.

The key to a park is to find one of significant size, such as D.C.'s Rock Creek Park, or Prospect Park in Brooklyn. Such territory can often be found along a river; the term "riverwalk" is a synonym for "banquet" in the vampire vocabulary. The second key, just as in finding a vampire's local territory, is to try to find a mark or bit of vampire graffiti in an archway, on a tree, or on a stone wall. Third, you've got to get in there at night.

Most parks close at dusk, and then are sporadically patrolled by rangers or rent-a-cops. So, map your route in the daytime, and find, in the daylight, a good nighttime entrance, one that's out of the way or well shrouded by trees, and make sure you can find your way after dark. You'll have to play it carefully, as there are human hazards in parks at night, but walk a route just as you would in town.

Don't skip those green places that aren't official parks or green zones. Scope these out when you can. Maybe there's a "rails to trails" biking and running path just on the edge of your city, or a body of water that isn't designated as a park but is a game management area.

## Industrial Zones

I once knew a vampire who had a simple but effective emergency lair: a large panel truck in a junkyard, a place where he could go if caught out too late. He had the whole thing outfitted for comfortable daytime rest. When staying there, his first hunting circuit for the night would begin among the warehouses and cement factory nearby.

Of course, these places are a bit more difficult to scout, as they're usually private property, and unless you're a hard hat, you'll look out of place here. But so what? Scout them anyway, looking for any sign that a vampire has tagged the area. Look for marks on buildings, stairwells, security fence posts, and loading dock doors.

The nice sort of vampires you're looking for oftentimes must make their homes wherever they can. Just because a handsome vampire doesn't go trotting out of his townhouse a short time after sundown, but instead emerges quietly and carefully from a loft space in an abandoned beer-keg storage facility doesn't mean he wouldn't or couldn't be the most refined fellow in your company. I've been on the move countless times, either on my own journeys

Believe it or not, some of the best vampire-to-human ratios have been found in Western cities, namely in Colorado, Wyoming, and New Mexico, with a lot of good-looking vampires and humans to boot. These areas have seen booming populations in the past twenty years, while they carry on a Western cultural tradition of high-and-wild adult fun. Frontier "lawlessness" often boiled down simply to people not giving a damn about what others think, including patronage of block-long communities of brothels. Prohibition in the West was a hell of a party, because those cowboys, both rich and dirt-poor, and everyone else would be damned if a bunch of bluenoses back East wouldn't let them have whiskey. I remember a place in Denver called Le Bonhomie du Frontier, a brothel and all-around fun house on the edge of the main part of town, in the early 1920s. An enterprising vampire could find just about anywhere to rest in the surrounding countryside, and have plenty of interesting women to woo, plenty of ambulatory food, and, in a pinch, a lot of livestock.

or on specific tasks with my coven, and while I have a few times been able to get a hotel room (hint: tip well), staying under the general human radar is a matter of course.

## Rural and Semirural Places

What if you live in a place with a much less dense population than the city dweller? How do you make yourself available in farm country, or forest, or the high desert?

As in more populated places, look around for vampire signs. In the countryside, these will, again, be seen on buildings, but you might also see signs on trees, posts, aqueducts, rock outcroppings, or bridge catwalks or pilings. These will be much farther apart than in a city or town. Map them and try your best. Also cast around for the most dense cover or structure near places where humans pass through; in essence, think like a predator perched over a game trail. If you notice a particularly thick stand of trees in a river bottom along a footpath that sees a decent amount of human travel, you might have spotted a lurking place.

But beware that you can run into a much rougher sort of vampire in the boonies. The reason being is that they rarely have to mingle among humans, or even try to pass for them. Those vampires that have suffered disfigurement, or those that have been banished from a coven, are often the vampires found in the country. Their existence is a bit more desperate, and they might be in hiding from pursuers of their own kind.

## Surviving First Contact

As you endeavor to bait a tiger trap with yourself, you must realize that you might attract a vampire seeking just to feed, and who most likely won't end your life, but won't have much to say to you either. You've been on dates like this before, no?

More than anything, a first encounter will be unnerving, either in its seductiveness or in its swiftness. A vampire who has trailed you carefully, and who has you in a location that's sufficiently deserted or concealed will usually attempt one of two approaches to bleeding you.

Some vampires will quietly call to you in a kind of whispering song that distracts your mind, slowing your movements and attentions, until he (or she) can sidle up to you and envelope you in his possessive gaze. You will find that something instinctive in you wants to move away at the same time that you consciously wish to embrace the dark stranger, but you will be unable to move or shout. The vampire will then wrap you up as smoothly as smoke.

Other vampires rely on speed, surprise, and strength, appearing out of the dark like an apparition to seize you tightly, overwhelming you. His eyes and face will strike you into silence, his constriction of your body forcing out any air you might use to scream.

Even though you are a willing victim, the first moment a vampire has you will provide terrific revelation—it might conjure every good and bad physical event that has ever befallen you. Women have told me that this thrill, such as it is, is always replicated just a bit every time I embrace them, and is a driving force behind their want to be taken and fed upon again and again. It is danger, desire, terror, excitement, taboo, sex, violation, need, and, indeed, love, all

Once, just before World War II, I was pursuing a well-to-do wife, at Christmastime, and watched her turn out the lights in the bedroom of her manse on the outskirts of Tarrytown; she had her own bedroom. I watched her gazing down at the moonlit snow for several moments before she drew the curtain, and I surmised what she was thinking. I emerged from the trees and leisurely made a lap of her high-walled home, where she was alone most of the time. She later told me her heart jumped when she saw my boot tracks in the snow, and again later when she saw a "B" in cursive script in blood in the side view mirror of her '36 Cord. Though I could have pried my way into her chamber that night, I wanted to give her a frisson of interest and pleasurable apprehension. That is central to the wooing of the blood.

rolled into one moment. It replicates an act of murder; an attack by a deadly animal; the female act of feeding someone; an act of survival—my physical survival, and possibly your psychological survival.

This strange meeting might be brief: You might have found a vampire interested in your warm, sweet blood only, despite your attraction to him. Regardless of your interest in this vampire, you must take his actions for what they are, and not become disheartened or self-hating if he does not express attraction to the rest of you beyond your blood.

You can, however, change a vampire's thinking. On the streets of south Philadelphia, not long after the War of Independence, I repeatedly encountered a lady of the evening, in a certain location, at a certain time, and fed from her on several nights, always leaving her when I was done. I paid her, surely, for I had taken up her time. Yet when she always asked, "Will I see you again?" she said so not in the voice of one hoping for more business, but in the tone of a woman interested. I scoffed at her question—I had barely any sense at all about what I was doing myself—but eventually, I came to realize she sought me, and one night I finally took a good look at her, and saw more clearly into her green eyes. I asked her name; she told me, and I became her consort for many weeks. Eventually, I helped her escape that town for a much better situation in Washington, D.C., where anyone can go to reform their career (she changed her name, married well, and forgot her past), and then I went forward on my own adventure.

But that woman proved to me that a human woman can influence a vampire, and make him look twice, if she is determined and willing enough. When she does, it's the beginning of something.

# The Wooing of the Blood, or, Will You Know When You're Being Pursued?

We gallant vampires often employ a much different approach, which is called "the wooing of the blood." We spot you and take quite an interest as you stroll along your circuit, having seen the marks we made to demarcate the perimeter of our coven's territory, or our immediate, individual space. But we need to make certain of you, to be sure you're not trying to "smoke us out" as part of a vampire-hunting team, or a reporter bent on getting the next great vampire story, digital camera at the ready. So we'll keep tabs on you, and we'll go to the places you go. We'll be about fifty paces behind you, but you won't see us.

You might catch the glimpse of a face at the window during a dinner party. Or you might see a small, odd mark scratched into the frame of your front door (the mark left by your vampire tagging your location, a message to others to stay away). You might think you see someone standing in a shadow by your car, where you parked it on the street, but you will dismiss this as a trick of the light and too much caffeine or wine, because when you get closer, the figure is gone. You might think this is the work of a garden-variety stalker, but there will be no direct contact. Yet.

Soon after, you might find a small indicator—a red velvet ribbon tied around your back doorknob, a crow's feather tucked neatly in the frame of your bedroom window, or a red marble in your mailbox. These might seem like pranks, and you'll ascribe them to people you know. But eventually you will receive a handwritten note, something simple, usually a message that will ensure a meeting: "Please go about your usual Thursday night routine."

Then he will reveal himself to you. He will find an opportune moment when you are alone, usually outdoors, where any other people are at a distance. He will suddenly be in front of you the way a wild animal can suddenly appear as if out of thin air. But he will not grab you, or attempt to feed from you. He will introduce himself, and ask to walk with you.

Your reaction is key. Even if you don't think he's "perfect," or your ideal of a vampire, do not shy away. This, after all, is what you've been trying for, and now he has shown himself in as innocuous a way as possible (for a vampire). If you shrink from him, either out of surprise, fear, or disappointment, he will most likely not pursue you, as he's taking the soft touch approach with a woman whom he likes specifically. That is, perhaps, the best definition of the gallant that I can give you: He is the vampire who will not press after you if you do not wish him to do so. But that will not be so easy if you do, in fact, attract him intensely.

Ideally, you will be inclined to him, and you will meet a number of times; he will approach without your knowing, singing or whispering to you, lulling you before he appears to you, but he will not yet drink your blood, because he wants you to reach your comfort level with him and with the idea of taking your blood. He will speak of drinking it, and he will ask how you might prefer him to do so—fang, dagger, or otherwise—but he will continue to court you. Years ago, of course, courting was in anticipation of marriage. Here, courtship is a ritual of increasing attraction, to the point that you can accept what he must do as a vampire to love you.

## The Beginnings of a Vampiric Romance

Being used to mortal men, and their natural state of confusion, ineptitude, conflicting messages, and dirty laundry, you will have little comprehension of relations with a vampire when the affair begins. You will be quickly schooled.

Let's assume for the sake of this discussion that your vampire is highly attracted to you and is willingly deferential to certain needs you have; he is as gallant as a vampire can be, and not the

I think perhaps the closest I ever came to death in my years as a vampire was at the hands of a jealous human boyfriend who was a mechanic and inventor. He had a sister who was overly involved in his life, and who often visited his home, where he lived with my girlfriend (who was, *ahem*, also his girlfriend in name). The sister several times observed my girlfriend leaving the house at night, and followed her, discovering that she and I met in an old barn. Now, whether the sister also figured out what I was up to is in question, but the insanely jealous boyfriend, who had watched *Terminator* way too many times, rigged

carry-you-off-and-possess-you type. But at the same time, your attraction for each other intensifies quickly. There are a number of factors to which you must adapt.

One, you will have to accept a certain amount of unpredictability in your evenings. You and your vampire will work out a meeting place and time for your trysts. But given the hazards of life up a homemade flamethrower with which to flash fry the interlopor. He came mighty close, and if it weren't for the clanking sound made by the hoso and tanks he carried, I might not have so readily dodged him. As it was, I had to scoop up my woman and scamper, as we had been caught in flagrante delicto, and dash into the tall grass while ducking hot bursts of homemade napalm. The boyfriend meant to flush us out of the field, but, running after us, he fired the flamethrower off balance, knocking himself on his back, and the burning slush of napalm went straight up and came right back down—right on him. He escaped with just a few bad burns, and I lit out for other territory.

in the blood state—the chase for prey and food; the constant need for a workable camouflage; random dangers presented by other vampires or human vampire hunters— you must allow for a certain amount of chaos. He'll sometimes come early, when you don't expect him. Other times he'll be late, leaving you to wait for hours, but not on purpose.

Second, your social and professional life will change. You will not be able to keep some dates. You will disappoint some people. If you often work late, your workflow will be interrupted occasionally. Friends and family will think you've become a little strange. If you're a single mother, you will have to make some careful babysitting arrangements.

Third, your love life will become a double life, if you have a husband or human boyfriend. This is the most complicated thing of all—to cleave to both human and vampire males simultaneously. The vampire will more often than not simply tolerate your human romance, as there's no point in causing much fuss as long as he's your one and only vampire. Mortal men, however, tend to behave as if they've lost their minds when they find that their woman is having a vampiric affair.

But there will be many ways in which to enjoy the blossoming of this romance. You will be the object of an irresistible desire; your vampire will pay great attention to you when in your presence. The mere scent of your skin, nearly synonymous with blood, will entrance him. Do not think of yourself as food. You possess his sustenance, physical and emotional, nearly one and the same.

You will quickly learn to enjoy his mouth on your opened vein as he pleasures you with his hands and body. Your first several acts of intercourse will be like no other sexual initiation you've had, as he will quickly sense the touch that brings you to orgasm, and then take you over that brink several times. His climax will occur only after a vigorous tending to you, and a good quantity of your blood is transferred to him.

You will enjoy your giving yourself over to his physical dominance, as if you had jumped in a river and let the current pull you along. But he can finish feeding before he finishes with you, and he will let you possess him—sit astride him, tie him, command him—when he is sated. Just understand that once you have allowed him to feed upon you, he simply cannot keep himself from tasting your blood soon upon encountering you. You can take your time with a cleansing ritual, and any other patterns or gestures you might enjoy, but be well aware that these initial efforts are the foreplay of bloodletting.

You will know that he worships your womanliness. I can attest to this. Every woman I have as a vampire ever been with had me enraptured with everything that made them female, and to know the blood that I drank flowed through every part of their femininity—their heart, their sex, their breasts, their legs, their mind—made me feel as close to them, even part of them, as any sexual act.

Such an intense connection would, one might think, bond a vampire to his human lover for a long time. In many cases, it does. I have carried on with just one woman over a course of years (albeit while I fed on many other humans). The trouble comes from the semi-immortal part, and other factors of a vampire's existence. We're very taxing on you ladies, and I beg your pardon. If we're not going to convert you, and you can't run away with us as a human adventurer and vampire consort, then what shall you do with us?

I say, enjoy us while you can.

## The Articles of Romance

A vampire will never commit to paper anything that could identify him as one in the blood state; he will never make a mark of vampire graffiti on paper, or write his name (he will use a nickname in writing). When he speaks on the phone with you, you cannot let slip any words that suggest anything about his inability to cavort bareheaded in the sun or his need for blood, because it's a given that a vampire-related vocabulary will get snooped out by security forces monitoring the phones with software that "listens" for such words.

But this doesn't mean your vampire won't leave notes or gifts for you. He will do so frequently, as a way of letting you know he is near when a visit isn't possible, or to leave you with something to think about until your next meeting. These mementos will be tucked where you will find them, but you might not readily see them,

although they will be left in your home; or outside, on a porch; or in a private place nearby, such as a garden. He will always leave these missals and presents in the same place, or close.

Flowers carry no identifying mark of he who gave them, and vampires are inordinately fond of flowers, as the transformation from bud to flower is symbolic of the transformation from human to vampire. And given the vampire's ability to obtain things readily, don't be surprised by the quantity of flowers you might receive.

Beyond these, vampires well understand the importance and symbolism imbued in those odd things that you and other people like to collect: marbles, sea glass, skulls, feathers, rocks and raw gem stones, dolls and toys, crosses and crucifixes (they don't bother us), and pins and buttons. We will give you these things to remember us.

## Vampire Vulnerabilities

Aside from the usual physical dangers—sunlight, buckshot, stake through the heart—there are other, more personal vulnerabilities inherent to a vampire once you've met him. These issues often hinge on the level of trust you attain with this fellow.

The first vulnerability has to do with his feelings about his past as a vampire. We blood drinkers are not all above or beyond feelings of guilt and regret over things we might have done to survive, especially in our earliest stages when we still thought and felt like humans, but were ostensibly vampires. We have those things we wish to keep quiet about, and those things that still scare us despite what great strength we have now. They say every vampire has a haunted soul. And we are vulnerable to human accusations of violence, monstrousness, and predation when such charges hit a sore spot.

We are vulnerable about past loves—women whom have long since died, or romances that failed because of our being what we are. I'm not the first vampire whose interests in a human woman resulted in her getting a great deal of negative attention from her peers, family, or constabulary; such cases are quickly hushed up, as the woman is forced to confess to delusions and wantonness, sometimes leading to the sanatorium, while the vampire is hunted or killed. We have our own versions of *Romeo and Juliet*.

We are made vulnerable by our hunger. Humans are difficult prey, made all the more difficult in an era of extensive forms of personal identification and security, forensic sciences, and boundless state security. Entering into a relationship with a human woman means for us that in bad or lean times, we know for sure we have some source of nutrition, however limited because you can give us only so much blood. Or, you can at least provide for us a secure place from which to observe and make quick forays to a victim, to whom we will assure you we won't cause undue harm.

We are made vulnerable by our need for security and secrecy. On our own, or away from our coven house, we rely on our wits, but also on you to give us a place to rest and relax, to recline and enjoy you. We have to believe that you will keep us a secret. But many a vampire was betrayed by a woman who thought she had been scorned, or who under great human duress gave up our resting place to those wonderful people with the wiretaps and Teflon stakes.

Finally, we are made vulnerable by our love of and need for you. Having a woman in our life greatly changes our habits. What we do, we do for the sake of sustaining our romance. When we venture forth at sundown, we will be considering the ways that we can get to you swiftly, at the exact time, and do so without leaving a trail. A vampire who has a steady human girlfriend knows such sustained interaction can expose both him and her to the watchful eyes of antivampire factions. Also, a vampire that simply feeds upon humans is left to fully engage all those things vampiric, including all activities of his coven. We romantic types do not always experience all that we could with our brethren, and this can make us vulnerable within the vampire community.

## Vampire Ambivalence

Amid the memories of human desire and the have-it-all power of being a vampire, a fellow such as I can get caught between enjoying a romance with a woman and the pull of the blood state. The result is a creature who greatly desires a romance with you but is hard put to give up the thrill of roaming the world and ruling nearly everything human that he encounters. This can dissipate his thoughts, his focus, and his dedication to the habits of human love. He'll still enjoy the blood and sex, but fail at the "you and me" parts of the relationship.  And even drawn as hotly to you as he might be, he will wonder if a relationship with a human weakens his existence as a vampire.

But such thoughts occur in the mind of a vampire who does not yet understand his full power, and that he can, indeed, be all the vampire he can be, and still have and enjoy a woman to whom he is wildly attracted. You can help stir his thoughts when he has these momentary, existential blues.

# Vampire Spying

All lovers occasionally spy on each other, mostly out of curiosity, and a wish to see how the person you adore acts away from your presence. This is, perhaps, a venal sin, though often it arises out of intense if mismanaged desire.

A vampire will sometimes shadow you to derive the pleasure of knowing he can protect you, and be at your avail without you knowing. If he senses you might have problems or be in any kind of conflict or danger, he might spy upon you if you go out at night. He also has a self-preserving reason for spying: He wants to see with whom you associate. Once he learns who your friends are, he will be able to recognize those people whom you trust, but also determine if he knows of them for other, not-so-pleasant reasons.

Your vampire cannot spy upon you for very long, as he has other things to tend to, but once he is aware of your nocturnal routines,

The social scene in Washington, D.C. in the early spring of 1961 was about as heady as it might have ever been, including the early Obama Administration. I was dating a very smart, sly redhead named Vanessa, who worked at the National Gallery as an archivist. One night, I spied on her, following her first in my car, and then on foot in Georgetown to an address on Cambridge Place. Curious, I lingered across the street, and noticed a large number of what I took to be Secret Service agents milling about the doorways. I found a good watching post in the shadows of the opposite building, and soon saw the reason for all the security: Mr. Allen Dulles, chief of the CIA, who emerged from a black Lincoln and casually strolled in the front door with just one bodyguard. I later found out that this was his birthday bash, just ten days before the Bay of Pigs debacle that brought about his resignation. Dulles had personally invited my Vanessa, as she had served as an adviser on a number of top secret cases that she refused to discuss with me.

both at home and on the town, he can at least make a good guess as to your location at any given moment, which is a comfort to him. He also knows where to go for the sake of seeing that you get home safely, if you and he don't already have an agreement for him to escort you. Believe me, you will have no idea he's there, if he doesn't want you to. Don't bother yourself with this. It's just what we do.

## The Woman's Controls

You might think that a vampire is so irresistible that even the nice one you're involved with is beyond your actual power. You can ask him to do things a certain way, but you don't think you can actually *make* him. Fear not, because just as your wiles work on human men, so, too, do they on my kind.

## Refusing Us Your Blood

One of the ethical pleasures of a relationship with a human woman is that the vampire is given blood, which to our minds is a very endearing and erotic kindness. It goes to the heart of whatever sense of honor we might have, because we know that the woman takes us at our word that we will love and protect her.

But if for some reason we run afoul of you, mistakenly or cavalierly, you can withhold your blood. In fact, if you really want to get our goat, swear you'll never let us taste your blood again, and that if we want to drink it, we must take it by force. That is something we cannot bring ourselves to do, not after having lovingly imbibed from your volunteered body. Whatever wrongheaded thing we've done we will quickly attempt to correct.

## Making Your Blood Unsweet

As a bit of a corrective, or a nasty surprise in response to some slight misdeed of ours, you can make your blood unsweet. Eating a combination of certain spices and foods can do this, and I won't name those things here because you have to figure this out. Well,

I'll give you one hint: Don't eat curry and wormwood at the same time.

## Physical Rejection

Saying you no longer take pleasure in your vampire's body is a harsh thing, because our physicality with you, from our mouth on your skin to our bodies pressed to yours, is central to our romance with you and our taking sustenance from you. The idea that physical contact no long holds any charge because you have some dispute with us will quickly bring about a resolution.

## Renounce Our Protection

This is tantamount to a breakup (see chapter 7), because renouncing our protection of you has a formal cast to it. It's really a way of saying, "Get out of my life, because I don't need you and don't want you to be you around me." Of course, as an ultimatum, it works, because a gallant vampire whose protection is rejected is akin to a cop whose badge has been taken.

# 4

# Getting It On

Unless a vampire finds you specifically interesting and starts pursuit of you himself, many months might pass before you yourself knowingly and actively get close enough to a vampire that he turns his head, so to speak. But all those efforts, if well aimed, will have a tremendously sensual payoff.

So far, I might have given you the impression that you and your vampire will simply collide in a splash of blood in your sexual meetings. You will surely enjoy such moments, but vampires do take pleasure in many of the trappings and habits of human sexuality. Vampire-human sex is a propagation of life, the vampire's life, while it is also a creative exercise, mingling the human with the formerly human.

# What Turns on a Vampire (Besides Blood)?

This is by turns a personal narrative—I can tell in certainty what *I* like. And I can tell what I have seen or heard other vampires like. What I discuss in this section are initial pleasures—those that come early in your sexual congress, and early in your romance before you move on to deeper stuff, which I'll discuss later. Of course, there are those vampire-seeking women who are ready to hang naked on the wall upside down on the first date. I believe you call these types "thrill seekers." Nothing wrong with that.

First, you must establish how well you communicate with your vampire. More than likely, he will tell you all that he believes you need to know. If you want to know more, demand it. On top of that, if there's something you want or like, ask for it. Vampires admire directness, even sharpness of tongue.

While we vampires can have as particular or odd tastes as any human, there are a number of universal vampire turn-ons that are also mutual, woman to vampire. You both can enjoy:

1. **PHYSICAL RESISTANCE:** A lively woman who leads us on a wanton chase around the house and puts up a spirited, albeit false, fight is most enjoyable. Chasing you down arouses something of an ancient predator in us. Such romping can dissolve into a merry

wrestling match. So don't give in too easily if your vampire man is willing to play. The exertion gets our blood flowing, enhancing the delivery of any that we might drink from your lovely body.

2. **SWINGS OR HAMMOCKS:** Rocking and swaying while we feed makes the blood slosh inside us, a very enjoyable sensation, and improves circulation. Such pendulum motion can also help our coital maneuvering with you, more comfortably bringing you to orgasm given the vigorousness of vampire sex, and impart a swooning sensation as your blood level drops.

3. **A SPECIAL ROOM:** As vampires no longer live with or among humans, in general, the idea of having a special, even secret chamber within your home that is reserved solely for our meetings with you is highly pleasing and exciting to our mind. Our safety is always in question when we're in your world, in your structures and homes. So knowing that this room is secure and a bit remote puts us at ease.

4. **SPECIAL LINGERIE:** Certain styles of clothing are designed tongue-in-cheek for the vamp-loving human crowd, and feature straps and materials that affect your blood flow—and heighten your vampire's pleasure. In many cases, the designers of such fashions are actually vampires. I can think of a specific example of such a thing: A latex catsuit worn by a wickedly kinky British expat for our meetings in Manhattan had cuffs above the elbow,

at the top of the neck, across the thigh, and around the midriff. Such effects can also be achieved with thongs of leather or bands of silk as well, these incorporated into various outfits. Of course, a getup that accentuates your natural assets is always a turn-on.

5. **EXHIBITIONISM AND PUBLIC DISPLAYS OF AFFECTION:** I was once standing at the corner of Haight and Fillmore, in San Francisco, waiting for a true California girl named Karina. She came marching up Haight in cowboy boots, an old Stetson, and a see-through nightie. Of course, this was the Lower Haight at one AM in 1972, but it was still a bit startling, and wildly exciting. The reason being is that your transgressions of typical public decorum draw attention to you, and thus, to your vampire. You actively take the risk of having the finger of authority point at him. But he will thoroughly enjoy your flaunting typical rules or fashions, while at the same time flashing yourself, and indicating that you don't mind taking your adventurousness up a notch. Additionally, the thrill of "getting caught" in public is much more profound for a vampire. Such potential troubles didn't stop me from taking Karina under the trees in Golden Gate Park, and it jangled my nerves enough that I still remember it clearly.

6. **SAUNAS:** A sauna or very hot bath, enjoyed in a place of very warm air, can actually aid our circulation, and thus accentuate our enjoyment of feeding and making love to you. Such heat

will also increase your circulation, making you all the more pleasurable.

7. **PLEASURING THE WOUND:** An army of Freudian analysts could spend the rest of their careers comparing the vampiric act of pleasuring the wound to both kissing and cunnilingus. Have at it, dear PhDs. But if you like how the vampire puts the hot tip of his tongue inside the bite or slit, he likes it just as much. Tell him to do it again.

8. **MASSAGE:** A vampire can enjoy giving you a massage, and will certainly enjoy you giving him one after he has fed, as this will aid the circulation and absorption of the blood he has imbibed. So if you like kneading your lover's limbs and muscles, then have at it, after he has fed, either from you or someone else. You might both incorporate some of those lotions that give off heat as you rub them in. Rough massage with the hands or abrasion with an object (a certain Asian skin-rubbing technique using a coin comes to mind) can also be a mutual turn-on. Maybe throw in a spank or two.

9. **ACTUAL BUT LIMITED PHYSICAL COMBAT:** If a woman actually has the chops—she's a karate black belt, or an expert at Krav Maga—she might unleash her force upon her vampire just when things are getting interesting. Anything that gets the blood pumping and acts as challenge to a vampire's physical prowess

is enjoyable to him. But do so knowing you will never beat a vampire, and might break a lot of furniture.

## When Less Is More

There are those times, despite all the accoutrements and manufactured sensations that can accompany feeding and lovemaking, that a vampire simply wants you. All you must do is stand in front of him and pull away your clothes to offer an exposed neck or arm. This is a nearly sacred gesture. It can bring your vampire man to his knees. It reaffirms your feelings for him, and in turn brings his expression of devotion to you. No public escapade, no specially designed corset, no secluded bathhouse will match the pleasure and importance of the act of feeding, and there are times when the centrality and purity of the act of nourishment and intercourse are all you need.

## Mutual Complications

The human-vampire bond is never a perfect physical and personal match, and that can create minor if brief distractions from or complications to your private endeavors. Some you might have to ignore, or get used to, while others you can try to modify.

1. **THE VAMPIRE BODY:** Our body temperature is 2.4 degrees Fahrenheit lower than yours, and our skin tends to be not as supple or soft. Naked, against you, we might feel a bit foreign. So try keeping your rooms extra warm, or include a hot bath or sauna in your romantic evening to warm up the vampire skin. There are also lubricants and lotions that generate heat when rubbed in. A vampire can also indulge as much body lotion as possible (we tend to do so, depending upon climate, and our skin does absorb it) to present the nicest a bodily surface possible. Warming us up is your pleasure.

2. **PHYSICAL OVERPOWERING:** Vampires are used to a tough physical world and are duly aroused by physical engagement. So you might find that in your first few intimacies, your vampire handles you without as much gentleness as you like. Just make him aware of this—everyone has different limits—and he will adjust the strength he applies accordingly.

3. **PAIN TURN-OFF:** Some women just don't like the pain of the vampire bite or stab. This pain doesn't last long, but it can have a negative affect on arousal. Your vampire could simply find a way to mesmerize you while readying to feed, and draw off enough of your attention so that the dagger seems more like an pinch. He might also make the cut quicker; so quick that you don't know it happened until it's over.

4. **SCARS AND MARKS:** No vampire wants to mar your skin with scars and marks, and surely you're even more concerned about this than he is. Be sure to insist that your vampire make very specific and small holes in the most inconspicuous places that still allow sufficient blood flow. He'll know these locations on your limbs and body. Secondly, be sure your vampire finds one or two locations that always bleed well, and these he can go to frequently. But there is a finite number of times he can puncture the same spot before such a mass of scar tissue builds up—a small but thick spot—that further penetration will risk tissue breakdown. Minimal tissue impact should be your vampire's goal.

5. **LOW BLOOD LEVELS:** If you are significantly underweight for your height, give blood often, or regularly have a heavy period, you might experience various blood level complications if your vampire feeds from you frequently in a short time. If you completely konk out during or just after letting your vampire feed, you need to find a way to boost your blood supply. Mostly a change in diet and exercise (boost both) are the remedy. Before you grumble, think of it this way: Having a vampire lover will put you in tip-top shape, if you do it right.

6. **SLEEP DEPRIVATION:** Even vampires must sleep. And a sex life will go to hell if one or both lovers are chronically drowsy. No one

wants to schedule sex like business meetings. You will both have to adjust your natural hours, sometimes giving and sometimes getting a compromise. A doting vampire lover will not want you to tire yourself out, and periodic stress affects the blood, too. Additionally, much human romance occurs after sunset. You'll manage it.

7. **COMPATIBLE SEXUAL LIMITS:** A vampire isn't one to shy away from swinging from the chandelier, so to speak. He might, in fact, start there. You, on the other hand, might be lustfully obsessed with desire for a vampire lover, but physically all you really like is basic and minimally athletic, and you don't yet have the nerve for adventurousness. You have to draw a line for yourself, and make that clear to your fanged lover. He will try to work with these limits, but you can expect him to try to induce you to some novel fun. Don't be shy. After all, your boyfriend drinks blood.

# Sexy Surprises for Your Vampire

Surprising a vampire isn't easy, but you can do it. Vampires actually do like surprises, just good ones, not bad ones. Finding out that my daytime resting place somehow made it onto the GPS in your cell phone is definitely a *bad* one. You whipping up a bunch of blood candy for my birthday—that's a very nice surprise.

So let's consider some good, very sexy surprises that you can use to your advantage, but don't limit yourself to what you read here—these can be a starting point for something even wilder:

1. **LEAD HIM ON AN OUTDOORS CHASE:** At an established meeting place, leave him a note or clue that sends him to a second location, where he will again find a written clue as to where you have gone. Then be polite and wait for him at this third place, but you might e-mail him scintillating photos of yourself to his cell phone while you wait (of course we use cell phones—you've no idea how important digital technology has become to our survival). If you're hard-core, however, this chase could be strung over several nights. Just be prepared for a teeth-rattling tango when he finds you.

2. **DRAW A CORDIAL OF YOUR BLOOD:** While you don't want to deprive him of much of the pleasure of feeding, you might draw a tiny bit of your blood into a cordial glass and have this ready for him upon his arrival (ask him beforehand to show you how to use a knife ever so carefully). He can drink it while you further impress him with some sort of other talent. Perhaps you're a contortionist?

3. **A HIDDEN TALENT:** Did I ask if you're a contortionist? Or a knife thrower? The headier and more physical, the better. Bellydancing? The balance beam? A rope dance? Vampires rarely have their physical prowess and talents matched or challenged, so if you've a unique physical ability which you've kept from him, whip it out some night. It will be quickly adapted to your foreplay. Vampires know how.

4. **MAKE HIM FIND YOU:** Invite your vampire to meet you amid a festival or holiday parade. Wear a disguise or costume and tease your lover into sensing you and then finding you. Vampires always indulge costumed human revelry, both for its helpful camouflage (we get to dress up like you dressing up like us) and potential nutrition.

5. **LIGHT-PROOF A SPECIAL ROOM:** Give your vampire a very safe, wholly dark place to rest once the sun comes up. Then make a room totally dark—as black as night—with a very dark,

light-absorbing interior, with just one place where sun can come through and shine on a nonreflective surface such as wool, velvet, or a rug. Wake your vampire at a predetermined time and take him into the special room. The sight of a sliver of sunlight on the rug or curtain will give him a moment's caution, as it and the thin shaft of light from the bared space at the window will appear to him as bright and brilliant as a gold strobe light. The sun is the one thing against which vampires have few defenses, and being so close to its presence while yet safe in the dark creates an enjoyable frisson of emotion in a vampire. Even the tiny rays of light that reach his skin and eyes will be sharp, and he won't be able to stay in here for long, but in that time you can let him feed from you and engage you sexually mere feet from his greatest enemy, kind of like kicking death in the face.

6. **BRING HIM SOMETHING DANGEROUS:** A vampire is used to and expects dangerous things, and would rather keep them from you. But when you show up with a hazardous but highly useable gift—a submachine gun, a very good cutlass or machete, a rattlesnake in a basket—he'll find you that much more intriguing and enjoy your sense of humor, too, for being willing to find and tote such a thing. (In this day and age, vampire covens possess numerous firearms for protection, and individual vampires frequently carry a fighting blade in addition to their dagger.

Once, I received a note from a lover that read, "Royal and Dumaine, Feb. 16." I knew that was Mardi Gras. The pickings were so easy in that throng that when I finally found my woman in her room at the Hotel Provincial, I was so well fed that I had to warn her that she was about to be shaken thoroughly. Another time, an oil heiress came by in her four-by-four truck and snatched me out of the abandoned ranch where I was residing, and without any hint of her plan, she drove for miles through the dark, overland, until we came to a mesquite patch along a creek. There stood a herd of the greatest Black Angus in the world, full of bovine blood so rich it is a delicacy among some vampires, including me. "Go on, cowboy, rope one," she said. I roped and drank from three, and, she being Texan, I never once had to pause with her. Picture that: A tall, white vampire shagging a long, lean golden cowgirl in the bed of that four-by-four under the stars until the sun almost roasted me, surrounded by nothing but nowhere. God, I love Texas.

The rattlesnake? In the past, snakes have been used effectually and ineffectually as camouflage for a feeding gone badly: Drop the snake on the deceased victim, induce it to bite, and leave. Besides, we like to keep vipers as pets, as they seem like kin.)

# Keeping the Blood Flowing

Good sex, I've found, involves long stretches of little thought. I can't tell you how many women have asked me, "What are you thinking?" while we are physically engaged. They are often confused and disappointed when I tell them I'm not thinking at all. I didn't say I'm not *feeling*, not *smelling*, not *tasting*, not *heating up*, not *possessed*. But one of the pleasures of sex should be freedom from thought and logic. If you're actually thinking about something during sex—"A causes B which results in C, so I should do A"—then turn that brain off, dear.

But now I will sound contradictory when I say that there are things about sex that require thoughtfulness and creativity in the act. Suffice it to say that during sex, if you are thinking at all, you're thinking in an immediate, sensuous way about touching that, or putting this there, or kissing that, or grabbing that and doing such-and-such.

So this section is about things you should think and know before your initial coital encounters with your vampire. Then most of your thinking will have been dispensed with, allowing *doing*, motion without having to think.

## Vampire Erogenous Zones and Anatomy

Vampires are not significantly more endowed physically than a human male; what body parts they have as humans they take with them, and those parts don't increase in size due to transformation. However, due to our blood flow and muscularity, we vampires can keep it up for quite a long time and pleasure you as much as you want.

Those male vampire parts that are sensitive to your touch are nearly the same as with a mortal man, with most of the pleasurable nerve endings in the usual places—the head and shaft of the penis. The lips, tongue, and mouth are particularly sensitive to touch, warmth, and the sensation of fluid. If you are so inclined, tickle the prostate. Warming lube is always welcome for that, natch.

Vampire sperm is invalid. Yes, we're shooting blanks. That's the one cellular change that doesn't occur. Pregnancy is impossible.

Should you ask your vampire to use a condom? Good question. Given that vampires, in general, do not suffer the effects of bacteria or viruses, the risk is minimal. But could a vampire carry for a short time a virus caught from a human? Possibly. So, play it safe, just as you would with a human lover. Over time, as you establish a level of real trust, you can come back to this is if one or both of you would rather do without the latex.

## Direct Arousal with Your Vampire

The scent and taste of your blood combined with the scent and feel of your body will arouse a vampire to erection quite thoroughly, but you can also lend a hand, as they say. You can apply a firmer grasp and use a bit more friction than you might with a mortal man, but the firm-but-gentle approach never changes. Please, no bicycle pump demonstrations—it might be vampire flesh, but steel it isn't.

Orally pleasuring your vampire is also welcome. But fellating your vampire to climax might be a bit tough on the jaw and throat due to the inherent vigor of the male vampire orgasm. Don't be afraid to use your teeth a little bit. Seriously, in certain famous brothels in Italy, the girls are taught a variety of fellating techniques, including those that involve deft work of the incisors on the head of the penis.

## Feeding During Sex

Your vampire will mostly likely need to feed from you very soon into your endeavors, mostly likely as soon as he can—as soon as you're behind closed doors or out of the way. But then he will suspend his feeding to enjoy the sensation of your blood inside him, and the sensation of your body and your lovemaking. But as he approaches orgasm he will probably again go to your vein, as the sensation of drinking and tasting your blood at climax is what he is really aiming for. The inward rush of blood and the outward rush of climax create a thrilling, terrifically *alive* feeling, I can tell you. But your vampire will not hurry to his orgasm, if you have time to enjoy each other, and will tend to you most fully, as your orgasms create a rush of blood to your sex, a sensation that is pleasing to him.

Don't be surprised if your vampire feeds from several different spots during intercourse—your neck, wrist, or inner thigh. A vampiric *soixante neuf* almost always involves the vampire drawing blood from the very seam of your leg, quite close to your vaginal opening, and so he can feed while he pleasures you.

But how, you ask, can he make his incision with all the shifting and bumping and humping? Very simple: He will say, "Be still, my dear," and for just a second, you stop your motion, and you will then feel the sting of his fang or dagger, and then the squeezing of his hand or fingers—all this in a matter of seconds—and then he will say, "Oh, yes," and you will feel his mouth on the wound.

You will not accidentally roll onto his dagger, or jar his fangs loose, or suffer a toothy tear in your skin. Accuracy is the name of the game when drawing blood during the deed.

## Enjoying the Wild Side

I'm not really sure there is any other "side" to a vampire romance except the wild side. It's *all* good, as they say, and it's all *wild*. Why else would you be doing this?

In fact, I find that within those women who have sought a vampire lover, and found me specifically, there is some uncontrollable desire to break out of a habit of being, be it social, sexual,

or personal, and embark on some kind of sexual epic. I think this comes from deep within that which is womanly, for to be in the female state is to have and enjoy a greater sexual prowess than men, such as Tiresias told us. Men, grand soldiers and statesmen that we might be, are limited by our hydraulics, so to speak. This talk of the multiorgasmic male, or the man who can have the forty-five-minute orgasm, is a stretch of the Tantric imagination. A woman, however, can have multiple orgasms; i.e., she contains the neurology for an entire sexual narrative, chapter by chapter, every time she is engaged by her man, or her several men, or simply by her own hand. I don't know why women have evolved this way, but it makes them most suitable for a very determined, long-lasting, improbable, outlaw lover. Enter the vampire.

## Vampires Are Naturally Kinky

I can recall a time when there was no word for "kinky," but we knew what it was. Now, according to *Webster's 10th Collegiate Dictionary*, it means, "Relating to, having, or appealing to bizarre or unconventional tastes especially in sex; *also*: sexually deviant" (second definition). And unfortunately with language, defining one word means having to define others; in this case, defining *bizarre*, *unconventional*, and *deviant*. But given that sex isn't just sex for a vampire, but is both intercourse and feast, that combination tends to lead to acts that are celebratory and creative.

## Vampire Fantasies for Him and Her

Despite being a young vampire, I believe that I have witnessed or heard tell of every possible twist of the womanly sexual imagination. So when I am with a girlfriend, I invite her to act out whatever fantasies she entertains. You will find the same is true with your vampire: A wide-ranging freedom of sexual expression is usually just fine. So whatever sexed-up stories you've got in your mind should be let out now, while you have the chance. Every fantasy involves varying degrees of a few standard necessities—ropes, blindfolds, role-playing—that in and of themselves might be singular attractions. In my experience, I have found these womanly fantasies most at the ready:

1. **TAKING HER VAMPIRE PRISONER:** Ah, yes, the old standby. We could write a dissertation on the theme of incarceration. I'll simply give you these guidelines: Do tell your vampire that you want to do this, and clearly demarcate the moment he is in your custody and is to do what you say. Don't fool around with the waning dark—liberate your vampire soon enough that he can return to his lair, if he must. Please let him feed first, before you

shackle him, and then do what you will. Also, if you really do mean to secure him so that he truly cannot escape (hint: you'll need chains and floor cleats), you will be replicating an old method of killing a vampire: chaining him completely to await the sun. If he lets you do this—say, chain him to a radiator while you tease him with various displays of self-pleasuring—you do indeed have his trust.

2. **BEING TAKEN PRISONER BY HER VAMPIRE:** The other half of the incarceration fantasy. A vampire can do this in any number of ways: He can use a variety of materials to tie you to the bedposts. He can lock you in a room that only he can enter and exit. He can wrap you up with one leg and one arm, and pin you to the bed or ground. And, as I have seen in some covens, there are iron maidens made specifically for sexual use. Your vampire might ask your preference, or he might surprise you. My best advice is to work out a code word for when you wish your imprisonment to end. Expect to be fed upon while held prisoner, otherwise there's not all that much pleasure in the act for your lover.

3. **TEACHING A VAMPIRE HOW TO FEED:** Every vampire had to go through a learning phase about feeding. Replicating that allows a woman a kind of nurturing control. Many women also enjoy the sensation of a vampire feeding from their arm, neck, or leg.

She then takes control of the vampire's rising arousal, giving him his initiation into the sexuality of feeding.

4. **ATTACK BY A MONSTROUS OR BRUTAL VAMPIRE:** This combines rape fantasy with the horror movie/monster fantasy, though a woman might enjoy either separately (sheer sexual attack, or consensual sex with a monster; both fantasies). The vampire can wear a mask or makeup replicating a disfigured or deformed vampire, and carry out a surprise assault on the woman, in which she will both delight in her repulsion at his appearance and her fear of assault. With or without any kind of costume, the vampire will handle his woman roughly, within the bounds set for indulgence of the fantasy. "No" is clearly not the right word here; a code word for "stop" is necessary. This is not a good outdoors fantasy, for once a gaggle of raccoon hunters nearly shot off my monster mask when they responded to my girlfriend's dramatic shouts while we enjoyed a midnight picnic.

5. **WATCHING HER VAMPIRE FEED:** Nearly every long-term human lover I have known asked for this form of consensual voyeurism. Sometimes they pointed out the woman for me while we attended a nighttime festival, while other times I told them how to catch sight of me, and let them try to figure out whom I pursued. This victim was not engaged sexually in any way; my girlfriend

simply watched me pursue, close in, hypnotize or secure, and then feed upon this victim, who was then left as safely as could be. This is not an easy fantasy to coordinate, and works well only in populous places where everyone is greatly distracted or involved in some mass public act (Burning Man, the Savannah St. Patrick's Day Parade, and the like). But I can still see the look on the faces of these women when I looked up at them with bloody lips, the limp body of another in my arms. The wild sex comes soon afterward.

6. **ALMOST BEING CAUGHT WITH HER VAMPIRE BY HER FRIENDS/ BOYFRIEND/SPOUSE:** You will at some point develop a strong desire for your entire world—friends, family, et al.—to know what a wild and grand time you are having. You will want them to see you, or almost see you, with your vampire. This is part ego, part taboo breaking, and probably part madness, but why not? Next time there's a family gathering or holiday party at your house, let your lover in through an upper window and ensconce him in just the right spare bedroom. You know the rest. Just be ready for the complaints: "Where do you keep going? You're missing your own party."

7. **PHYSICALLY DOMINATING HER VAMPIRE:** To what degree your vampire lets you dominate him is something you will have to negotiate. This can range from victorious wrestling to tying him

up (see number one), to the farther limits of bondage, but you'll test his limits of playfulness and humorous self-depreciation. But he'll be game for letting you tie him to the bed posts or ride him around the house like a pony if the rewards are right.

8. **BEING GIVEN A SECRET NAME AND IDENTITY:** Several times I have been involved with women who had an enjoyable time with me as themselves. But when each of them went through a symbolic transformation, giving themselves a new name, and new ways to dress, act, and approach me, the sex just took off. Becoming someone else is central to fantasy, and crossing this threshold makes all the difference with some women, possibly you. If you suspect you'd like to be somebody else, you and your vampire can turn you into her through mutual creation of the necessary steps. I often find that when this transformative act climaxed with a woman's tasting her own blood, and thus knowing what I tasted, she fit the new personality easily.

Your vampire will most likely harbor the following imaginative kinks, some left over from his human years, some derived from his vampiric experiences:

1. **CONVERTING SEVERAL WOMEN TO START A COVEN:** A vampire doesn't start a coven on a whim, but it's an exciting and sexy thing

for him to pretend to do. This would involve a little role-playing: The woman will have to take on the identity of several different women, and let herself be fed upon several times. You and the vampire will also have to mimic the last step of conversion— your drinking his blood. Use your favorite red wine.

2. **RESCUING HIS WOMAN FROM ANOTHER VAMPIRE:** Having had to do this for real, in the kind of intravampire competition that my kind indulges and endures, I can say that this does charge up the blood and make a vampire all the more aroused to have his woman in his arms again. A game of hide-and-seek can replicate this. When your vampire locates and "frees" you, you can describe the horrid depredations of the rival vampire, and your lover can describe how he dispatched the foe. Then celebrate your reunion.

3. **RECREATING HIS MOMENT OF CONVERSION:** This will take some explaining beforehand, and you will most likely play the role of the vampire who converted your man, or that of a human who rescued or found your lover without knowing he was turning into a vampire. The most scintillating part of this is recreating the moment your lover first fed from a human. For that, you might play the part of an unwilling woman who learns the vampire won't hurt her, but is just desperate to feed and needs her.

4. **REUNITING WITH A BELOVED WOMAN FROM HIS HUMAN LIFE:** If you can handle this without suffering any jealousy or

dislike, you could thoroughly excite him by playing the role of a woman whom he loved but lost after his conversion. You might have already been chosen because of your resemblance to her, and your secret name for role-playing might be her name. Life is twisted, no?

5. **THE WOMAN PLAYS VAMPIRE HUNTER:** Being hunted often strikes a vampire as a sporting challenge. It brings a disturbing thrill to a being who is otherwise very secure in his sense of going undetected. This, like other fantasies, will require some running room. You will initiate outside of any secret love nests you have, as you will have to begin by stalking your vampire, getting close to him, and putting him on edge (in an imaginative sense). You will, however, need to end up at a private location where you can "capture" him.

6. **HIS WOMAN VOLUNTARILY TURNS INTO A VAMPIRE ON HER OWN:** Egotistically speaking, as I can say for myself, a vampire involved with a human woman eventually assumes that he is the only vampire she knows, and if she were to be turned into a vampire, he would be the one to do it. So it can act as a startling and arousing violation of his ideas about you when you show up "in the fang gang," as we say. You're suddenly on par with him, and this can turn him on in any number of ways. And of course, you make for a stunning vampire in his

eyes. To pull off this fantasy, you'll have to surprise him with your own gear and getup, and be convincing. This one might start off with some verbal sparring a good while before you actually upstage Vampirella. You might start the conversation by asking, "What would you do if I was just like you? If I let another vampire convert me?" You're a good actor, right? Take it from there.

## Blood Fetishizing and Blood Bathing

You humans are a strange and excitable lot when it comes to your food. You eat too much of it, or you starve yourselves. You go crazy over cooking shows on television, and then eat unbelievably disgusting things engineered to taste like nothing natural. You enjoy food fights. You made Nutella underwear and ate it off each other in college, didn't you?

So don't be surprised at the way some vampires sexualize blood itself. Blood is life, and can easily take on a wholly erotic nature.

So you might find your vampire spreading blood upon you or marking with blood various parts of your body just before you get it on. He might do other things: Stain a small cloth or bandanna with your blood and keep it with him, and use it as a way of arousing himself before visiting you. Immediately spread your blood under

A vampire who travels as much as I do must be careful to operate under the radar of local covens (if not as their guest), and must always be on the lookout for their territorial markers. In general, I have succeeded; most established territories are well known and you don't go poaching in them for long. But once, while on an extended stay in San Francisco, my lovely Karina and I were holed up in an abandoned warehouse, when a pair of horrid, hulking creatures in black leather invaded our abode. They were ex-bikers, and vampires, who had followed us the night before and decided they didn't like my stepping on their turf. One leapt upon me, while the other carried off Karina. Only my combat experience saved me, and I managed to get this endomorph's machete away from him, and separated body from head. Moving silently, I found the other one on the street, using chains to lash Karina to him like a backpack so he could more easily drive away on his

> motorcycle. I was able to get close enough to get in one fast slash to his neck. Karina and I crossed the Oregon state line in a matter of hours on that fast Harley, and the exhilarated relief of having her, unharmed, again to myself was beyond description. I had quite a bit of difficulty hiding the bodies of those big bastards.

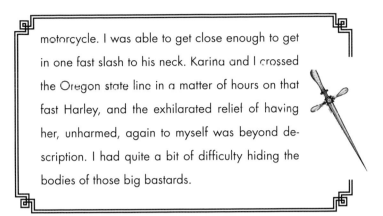

his nose or around your neck as he feeds so he can smell that blood during sex.

Another thing your vampire might enjoy is blood bathing. This is a fun, albeit gratuitous behavior that is not enjoyed frequently due to the sheer necessity of getting enough blood to fill a large bathtub, or even a Jacuzzi (in this case, a water-blood mix). Vampire skin can absorb blood to some degree, and bathing in it while drinking it aids in saturating the muscle groups. I myself have enjoyed a "nutrient high" through such a practice, which usually calls for using high-quality beef or horse blood, as that much human blood usually necessitates several dead people.

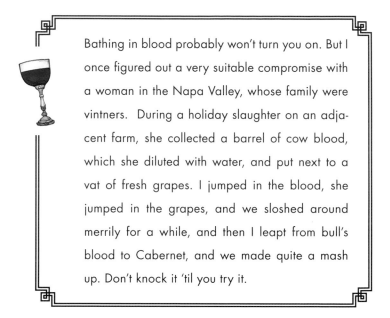

Bathing in blood probably won't turn you on. But I once figured out a very suitable compromise with a woman in the Napa Valley, whose family were vintners. During a holiday slaughter on an adjacent farm, she collected a barrel of cow blood, which she diluted with water, and put next to a vat of fresh grapes. I jumped in the blood, she jumped in the grapes, and we sloshed around merrily for a while, and then I leapt from bull's blood to Cabernet, and we made quite a mash up. Don't knock it 'til you try it.

You shouldn't be bothered by such things, odd or kinky as they might be. They are simply part and parcel of the vampire lifestyle. You've often heard a wine lover, or even a whiskey lover, talk about jumping into a vat of the stuff. We vampires feel the same way about our preferred beverage; whereas a blood bath or hot tub swirling with blood only serves to supercharge the vampire, a human in a vat of strong alcohol can quickly get incredibly drunk, then poisoned, and then drown.

As mentioned in "Mutual Complications," taking a dip in blood might not be your ideal romantic evening. And blood in such quantity could turn the stomach of the most stalwart human female, because blood does not smell good to the human nose. If this is the case with you, but your vampire turns out to be a bit of a blood fetishist, you're going to have to work something out that's sufficiently arousing to him without being too demanding of you.

# Bring Out the Toys!

Before, I addressed the idea of you taking your vampire prisoner, and vice versa. While that can be as simple as shutting someone in a room, it usually involves some sort of restraint, and often leads to the application of a crop or lash because the prisoner has been "bad." Oh my.

Your vampire most likely will submit to a bit of this play for the sake of enhancing his anticipation of tasting you. He might let you bind his hands to the bedposts, or entirely tie him up, or shackle him to the radiator or barn door, and then enjoy you happily flaunting your body and blood before him. And if it thrills you, he will let you spank or lash him, the little stings delighting him only in the sense that they will make more exquisite the flavor of your blood and sensation of your body.

Vampires don't get off on pain (at least, I don't, and I've not known any who did). We have a very high pain threshold, owing to physiological transformations that occur in becoming a vampire. And for some evolutionary reason, our bodies and brains sense real pain in much the same way an animal does: as wholly displeasing, negative stimulus.

But that does not mean your vampire won't indulge your kinky wonts. And if you  enjoy a bit of the lash yourself, your fanged lover will expertly apply it. The sight of skin turned scarlet by a spanking or a paddle, or the sight of whip welts turn a vampire on, because they make him think of the blood underneath that skin, and how warm and sweet it is. A vampire will happily raise a bit of a welt and rub it with his thumb until it's hot. But he will not mark you unduly or badly (think *Story of O*) because causing severe welts or bruises becomes overt and is a waste of blood. I only need to see a little of your corpuscular color let loose in your skin and I'm hot for you, and I would gather that most nocturnal fellows any human woman would find attractive think the same way.

## Threesomes and More

You will most surely surprise your vampire if you bring a friend unannounced to an assignation, and might surprise him a bit too much. As in the human threesome, trust is a big issue. If you think it would be fun to bring one of your girlfriends along, you might be right, but you need to evaluate this with your vampire before you do so. True—a vampire might not care if he arrives at your meeting place to find you and someone else he's never seen before sitting there on the bed (a lovely gal once pulled this stunt on me at the Chateau Marmont, presenting a wide-eyed young woman who looked like she'd been thrown out of Brian Jones's suite). He might not care if a random person finds out what he is, because he can easily scare her into silence; I've done so, and it's not pretty—it'll scare you, too. But out of respect for your fanged one, tell your boyfriend about the woman you've got in mind, because she's got to be as sporting and trustworthy as you.

But a vampire certainly does enjoy the occasional ménage à trois. You should, however, be as utterly certain of these penchants in the person you select as you are certain of them in yourself: Your friend must have the spirit and sportingness to wish to cavort with a vampire; have sufficient health and blood; have no fear of being fed upon; and have the utmost ability to keep it all a secret. Yet also be wary of picking someone who will seek to unseat you as your vampire's favorite one, for once she is so expertly and thoroughly ravished, and understands the power of a vampire in her life, she might very quickly decide that you, dear reader, need to get out of the way.

Now, what if you happen to have a human boyfriend, and wish to bring him, or any other man, along to your tryst with your vampire? To some vampires, blood is blood, and as long as your fellow fits the bill and you've handpicked him, then you can carry on. But don't expect your vampire to take any interest in your human boyfriend beyond drinking his blood. You must bear in mind that human men and male vampires often have a nature like dogs when face-to-face: They are territorial about the woman, are not attracted to each other, and would happily chuck the other out the window. As I have on a few occasions in the past, your vampire might tolerate without jealousy the sexual attendance of your boyfriend, feeding upon you while letting him pleasure you. He does this out of knowledge of the extreme enjoyment it gives you. But even vampires who left behind hetero-human lives have heterosexual limits, and behind closed doors I find men of no value besides their blood. They also tend to shoot their mouths off about their sexual adventures. You've got to be utterly certain that the boyfriend won't lose his mind about this, or loosen his tongue, for if he does *I will kill him*, says your vampire, because a vampire will be damned if he'll let some popinjay boyfriend put him at risk.

So, when it comes to multiple partners, as with other variations on straightforward sex, you've got to ask yourself what you'd like to do, what your vampire would like to do, and what either of you will tolerate. Your vampire might lust wildly for a threesome—you and any another woman—and yet you can think of only one other person, a friend, whom you would tolerate as the second woman in the bedchamber. So, why haven't you called her?

# Vampire Sex Magic

Having been around as long as I have, and seen what I've seen, the notions of the Kundalini, chakras, and nadis strike me as entirely possible. At times in my life, I have experienced feelings of energy within me that I could not explain, but I have sometimes felt blood absorption occur intensely enough in my body in certain places to suggest that somehow our bodies create zones of electrochemical force, and we can alter and affect these through intercourse.

I need not explain here the Kama Sutra or Tantric and Taoist sexual practices—that's another book. What I do want to say is that these practices, while not always possible, can be immensely enjoyable to the vampire because of their affect on circulation. Tantric sex, while being an entire spiritual guide, focuses in particular on the internal distribution of sexual energies that build before orgasm.

How you manage your orgasms is your business. But if you happen to be adept at various positions that allow you a great deal of physical control, use them. The breathing rituals common to the most basic Tantric sex practices are pleasurable to a vampire because they focus both woman and vampire upon coming into respiratory sync, which in turn helps the vampire focus on circulation and enjoy the feeling of the blood inside him being absorbed into different muscle groups. This pleasure is carried along by the Tantric method of building but not releasing orgasmic force (at least, not releasing it quickly), and thus it gives a vampire the full feeding experience. Through various muscle contractions, the vampire can force more or less blood to his lower or upper body and limbs. Having fed fully, and partly from you, your fanged man will arrive at a most engorged climax after a long Tantric session.

## Daytime Resting with Your Vampire

For reasons of security, a vampire will usually not tell you where he rests during the day. That's information you shouldn't know. Keeping himself secure while he slumbers is his business, not yours.

But on occasion, you can convince your vampire to let you stay with him in his daytime lair. At some point, your curiosity will have to be mollified. But you will be blindfolded, and possibly even drugged, as he conducts you to this place (something that in and of itself could be arousing).

Once there, your vampire man will fall into a deep but animal-like sleep—he can rouse very easily and quickly if he detects some-

thing awry. You can join him in this sleep. A number of women
in my life have asked to be able to lie with me while I rested, and
I satisfied their request. Women derive a very sweet pleasure
from "spending the night," or day, as it were, with their vampire,
curled up together in his place of rest. Just bear in mind that upon
waking, he will take you and feed upon you right then and there, as
he will not be able to stop himself. But this is the lovely pleasure
you're looking for isn't it—waking up together after long sleep, like
human lovers?

Your vampire will sleep in something very comfortable but also something very secure. To that end, if he has a long-established residence, he will have a sleeping chamber: A boxlike piece of furniture big enough for a sizeable mattress and pillows. Think of something like a cross between a coffin and a tent, made of wood, combinations of wood and metal, or even some sort of space-age polymer. These things vampires make for themselves, as during sleep they are truly vulnerable. The room in which the sleeping chamber sits will be lightproof.

Not all vampires have it so good. Some sleep where they can, in warehouses or barns, or even in the woods and forests, making use of camping equipment. I once backpacked across the country, and it was grand. And, yes, gorp-eating crunchies *do* taste like granola.

# 5

# The Vampire as Sex God

If you've gotten this far, you've certainly reached one conclusion: A liaison with a vampire is more demanding than anything you've known. It will blend all the heady and uncontrollable feelings of teenage love with your more practiced, mature sense of sexual self. You think about him more often than you want; you will close your eyes while at work and be able to feel his lips on yours, and his mouth on your skin. You will find yourself aroused at the most inopportune times by thoughts of the most salacious things.

Striking a balance with a vampire lover is difficult, because he cannot entirely change his way of life for you. He can alter his behavior here and there, and he will do what he can to match your needs even when they run counter to his tastes or instincts. But he cannot be in your life without existing as a sexually magnetic force that constantly draws your thoughts, heart, and body to him.

You can use the word *obsession* if you like, although in this context it should have a rather positive spin. Why disregard one sliver of such an intense sexual connection or the being that makes it possible? Let yourself be open to his potency and that which is yours when you are with him.

The trouble comes in trying to ascribe human romantic and sexual mores to your vampire and your relationship with him (that's not to say that you and he can't do so when you both find a habit of being that works for both of you). Vampires are not creatures with serious regard for human-made "rules." One's sex life is very different when you change from being an animal with a twenty-year breeding period in a seventy-two-year lifespan to one that can live for a thousand years and reproduce at will. So let's consider a few of these factors.

## Is Monogamy Possible?

Yes, and no. This works both ways.

Vampires live long, and thus forge long and lasting relationships within various vampire communities. Among these are long-standing relationships with other vampires, and these relationships can often have a sexual element. You'd be hard pressed to find that your vampire boyfriend does not have a few once-and-future female vampire lovers scattered around the globe. Such partnerships come and go, and are, on one level, purely recreational and focused on the mutual pleasure of feeding. But on another level, they can span centuries and involve all sorts of concerns about power and organization within vampire societies. This is where complications can occur because your boyfriend might have a societal or ritual obligation that calls for him to once again mingle with a female vampire he has known for years.

Vampire-on-vampire sex is different from what you have with your vampire man. While it can be excellent, it has nothing of the beautiful fragility, emotionality, and sweetness of relations with human women. This is one of the reasons why some male vampires covet their relations with their human lover, and can forsake all other human women for her.

That is something which you do have a right to ask for: that your vampire has just one human woman—you. He will most likely agree. But he will surely feed from other humans, both women and men, because he must. And he cannot always explain himself if he must disappear into a necessary activity with his coven or vampire cadres.

Then there's you. I've known talented women who managed to have both human boyfriends and a vampire lover simultaneously. And I've known a few wildly-talented women who had more than one vampire suitor, although not in the same room, at the same time—that would cause a bit of a fuss.

But what does your vampire have a right to expect from you? If he is to be your one and only, either human or vampire, then he can ask the same of you. A lot depends upon your situation and what both of you are willing to compromise. Most likely, he

Such massive slaughter occurred on the Eastern Front, in the fighting between the Third Reich and the Soviet Union, that entire populations in various regions were wiped out. Resident vampires had to move to find accessible, viable collections of humans, and while migrating these vampires began to fall prey to the extremely determined antivampire teams that the Soviets operated. Covens with Ukrainian connections stepped in, including mine, given our origins in Philadelphia's Fairmount section, which once had a large Ukrainian population and we, thus, took in a number of Ukrainian members.

won't concern himself much about human boyfriends as long as he knows you really love him. But your loving another vampire is out of the question, because the idea of another tasting and enjoying you and your blood will probably infuriate him. Don't interpret this as you simply being a demijohn of blood, both source and container of a precious commodity that he doesn't want to share. It's about you giving something to him that you give to none other but him: life.

During this operation, in which we resisted both armed Nazis and Soviets, a covenmate named Valdene, whom I had known years before, joined us to do her part. Seeing her again after several decades was a delight. I knew that within a short time, we would enjoy a repast of blood together, and then some. But after the months-long operation, during which we drank a good deal of Russian and German blood, my coven returned to the United States with a number of refugees. Valdene went back to her second coven in the Pacific Northwest (one she had started). I returned to a woman in New York, with whom I kept myself for a decade more.

# The Unstoppable Vampire Libido

Your vampire always wants you. As soon as he shows up, as soon as he smells your blood, and then—just as he wishes to taste it and while he tastes it—he is having you. This is a difficult routine to break. You might also feel yourself overwhelmed by it at times. But then again, why are you doing this? Not to play post office, surely, or some other game? You will find ways to modulate the vampire libido: Ask him to be well fed before he arrives so he doesn't devour you so readily. Have a ritual for meeting that must play out before he can draw your blood—a sequence of removing jewelry and garments that you wear for him only, or reading short poems or prayers per your tastes, or always beginning your encounter with a cleaning ritual, or a complete waltz.

You cannot, however, expect many meetings with your vampire that do not in some way include something sexual. He does not look at you as a sexual being only, or a "vessel," to be sure. But to be near you, to see you and smell you, is to want you. And, as I have said, the blood want is primal.

# When It All Seems Like Endless Seduction

All lovers are guilty of settling into patterns. Your trysts with your vampire cannot in and of themselves be boring, but after a while you might ask yourself if you will be forever locked in a pattern with someone who is not human.

You have indeed run upon the existential issue that all women like you face after they have become involved in this way for some time: What does it mean to your life to sustain an intimate relationship with a being who does not age like you, or reproduce like you, and lives on blood?

Every woman in love with her vampire will have to find her own answer to this question. I don't think I should try to answer it for you. But I can try in these subsequent chapters to give you insight in the ways of sustaining a woman-to-vampire relationship over a significant course of time. I have in my life in the blood state been involved with just one human woman for a number of years; in one case, for nearly forty years.

But I know what you want to know: What did that mean physically and emotionally for me to attend to just one mortal woman? It meant I had no other human lovers with whom I was in love. I fed from other human women during this time but did not make love to them while I fed. Many vampires would call me a fool for limiting myself so, when sex is to feeding as what chocolate bunnies are to Easter. But when not involved with a specific woman, I certainly indulge those women who, upon my approach, found themselves open to their sexual desires.

Could your vampire love you and just you for your entire life? Well, what do you mean by *love*? If you mean that he will hold you highest in his heart, and hope to be returned to you before your death or his, then, yes, he could surely do that. When I once found a cadre dying, and beyond any help, he whispered a very simple benediction: the name of his human love. I found that woman and told her that her lover's mind and heart raced to her in his final moment. That seemed to mean more to her than anything else.

But if by *love* you mean that for your entire life he refuses himself any physical sexuality with any other being, human or vampire, you will sorely press his limits. Even when you are sixty, seventy, eighty, or more, he will continue to visit you and love you, and taste your blood, if you can sustain that. But at that stage of your life, would you refuse him his necessity as a vampire to create the next stage of his life—that of his life in vampire society, and his personal life? And at the age of sixty-five, do you expect to swing in that midnight hammock atop your vampire?

Perhaps you do, and I hope that you will. Your vampire who loves you will be there, too. You are both still the same people, but one is aging, and the other is not.

Can you convince a vampire to marry you? Possibly. We'll talk about that later. But before we go rushing to the Blood Altar, let's get to the basics of maintaining this thing you've got going. This hot, crazy, wild-fun, orgasmic thing—yes, that.

# 6

# Becoming a Vampire Lover

So, here's what has happened: You went to the right part of town, at night, and put yourself on a regular circuit. Your vampire swain appeared and wasted no time in tasting your blood. But you lent yourself to the seduction; you looked into his eyes with a powerful mischief that made clear your interest. So you met again, and then again. And now you find that you have regular meetings, two or three times weekly, in secret, secure places, and he drinks your blood while you make love with him, and you're both in agony when you know he must leave.

Now what?

## Figuring Out the Nature of Your Vampire Relationship

I'm no great fan of categories. Everyone is in his or her own category. So what I describe here is a rough sketch of some widespread habits and natures of the human-vampire romance, something that you can use to help form a model of your own vampire relationship. Nothing is ever so tidy, but you might take the general form of one or a blend of the following

1. **STURM UND DRANG:** This is what happens when a high-strung vampire meets a high-drama woman (you know who you are). While this can make for a hot volatility that madly excites and pleasurably exhausts, it also can create a kind of intimate turbulence that eventually will make everything else difficult. Let's say you're a bit like Marla Singer in the film *Fight Club* and your vampire is a few degrees removed from that actor who's lately been playing Batman on screen, then you've got yourself a bit of "storm and urge." I can never figure out how these types always end up together, but they do, don't they?

   *HOW YOU'LL GET ALONG:* Have you and your vampire identify your three most dramatic traits or reactions and figure out a way to channel that energy constructively; always be aware of what makes you happy (or at least mellow), and how, and focus on ways to repeat those steps the next time.

2. **BLOODSPORT OLYMPIANS:** The couple that can never have enough sex and the vampire who can never drink enough blood. In another life they could have been world-class

downhill skiers or Iron Man competitors, but instead these two body-worshipping, physical elites set records for friction and blood given or imbibed. The Tour de France might have perfected methods of blood doping, but years ago European women who wanted their vampires to gorge on them would inject themselves with their own blood, drawn and stored a short time before the arrival of their fanged man, so that he could drink whole pints while the extra corpuscles supercharged her arousal. *Damn*, that's hot.

**HOW YOU'LL GET ALONG:** Don't try to outdo your vampire, and he shouldn't try to push you too far, endurance wise. Find a groove and work it for a while, then plan new challenges together.

3. **YOUNG NEWLYWEDS:** This is usually the romantic form taken by a very new vampire (who might be any human age) and a woman who is experiencing her first vampire after long contemplating the fascination without acting upon it. They're nearly relieved to have found each other, and are willing to stop right here. The vampire makes a beeline for her as soon as the sun has sunk beneath the sea, and she waits for him every sundown, everything neat and in its place in her home, everything about her dress and person perfect. They feast their eyes on each other when they meet, and the vampire

always asks for permission to feed, and then does so carefully, not drinking too much. There are couples like this who have been together for sixty years, and their pain at the end, when the woman dies, is unbearable.

**HOW YOU'LL GET ALONG:** Be candid about your tendency to put yourself in a bubble, and make sure this doesn't turn into isolation. On the flip side, this is the kind of relationship where converting the woman at a young age is a great temptation and probably the best solution.

4. **DOMINATION AND POSSESSION:** Nine times out of ten, this is a situation in which the vampire is in complete control of everything, the woman a (mostly) willing acolyte and consort. This is the habit of very old, very powerful vampires, and those vampires who tend to wickedness among their kind and near brutality with humans. But on occasion, the woman is the one in the seat of power, for she somehow has the personality to dominate her vampire mentally and emotionally. This usually happens with a very new vampire, and won't last long once he realizes his power. But it can occur with an established vampire who meets a woman who so madly reminds him of a lost love of his human years, that he submits readily to her will. There is some excitement in giving yourself over totally to someone

else, but this high register of personal lending cannot last long.

**HOW YOU'LL GET ALONG:** If the vampire is dominant, the woman is going to have to realize how long she can last under such control, knowing she might have to escape it. If the woman is dominant, she will have to expect that her vampire will eventually assert himself, and then decide if she can abide power sharing within the relationship.

5. **LONG AGO AND FAR AWAY:** Sometimes I see those people at Renaissance fairs in their chain mail and leather bodices, and have a bit of a laugh (and a drink). But some vampire couples indulge something similar. In this case, the vampire is usually some kind of history nut with a strong yearning for older vampire days when we had a much easier time, and the woman is a die-hard romantic who purposefully sought a vampire as a kind of Old-World swain who is open to her desire to wear period costume. They view themselves as a couple that is "out of time," removed from current history, living their own history in another time or parallel universe. These relationships can be particularly strong but they are bonded by fantasy.

**HOW YOU'LL GET ALONG:** Give in to it—your entire relationship is the stuff of fantasy. Every day is Comic-Con.

6. **GLAM AND SLAM:** This is the downtown couple deeply into a certain scene—punk, glam, steampunk, Burning Man, metal, hipster, mod, goth—that involves a lot of dressing up, makeup, dancing, and various intoxicants. Endless nightlife and specific costume provide excellent cover for the vampire, especially one who was transformed as a teenager or young adult. I've known of more than one occasion when the young woman didn't even realize her guy actually was a vampire. "I just thought he was really into biting," she says, when she realizes that after a couple months of dating they really never have ventured out in the daylight. Any number of these relationships have spilled over into marriages of designers, where the wife runs the business during the day, and the vampire designs the clothes and accessories at night. The "public husband" is usually a gay stand-in who knows everything but no one believes him.

   ***HOW YOU'LL GET ALONG:*** Have fun for as long as you can, but if you find yourselves finishing each other's sentences about fashion and design, you might be on to something. You'll end up collaborators (or more), or break up on the dance floor because his favorite playlist is so 2007.

7. **THE SOUL MATE:** A blood couple whose relationship forms a specific kind of refuge from their lives, and which often

involves a specific, secret meeting place where they can spend all their time. This meeting place hearkens back to something crucial from their past—a garden, a cottage, or a treehouse. They're able to connect with and deal with that part of themselves that might still be frozen at a certain moment in their young lives. Meeting in the same place every time is risky—it creates too much of a pattern—but it is a psychological necessity for these two.

**HOW YOU'LL GET ALONG:** This is psychoanalysis for two, but without the requisite professional therapist. You might find that crucial psychological breakthrough for each other, or you'll just play into each other's neuroses to the point that you can't relate.

8. **THE NOCTURNAL HUSBAND:** At about 10:45, you hear the door open, your man comes in, takes off his coat, says, "Hi, honey," kisses you on the neck, and you two sit down for a bit of a meal and talk about your day. And then he fixes things—the vacuum, the cabinets, the deck, even the car. You watch him through the window, smiling to yourself as you iron some of his shirts. Then he comes in, disgruntled at his failings as a carpenter or a mechanic, and you have a bit of a spat about meaningless things. But you quickly make up with some earnest, just-like-married sex and he's careful

I admit that I'm a bit of a questing vampire, but this has come out of my deliberate work as a national range spy for my coven, and because I tend to like physical adventure in the out-of-doors. Yet my most beloved woman, Jocelyn, was not much of an out-doors adventurer at all. She liked to garden, and she liked to go out in her carriage, but anything involving climbing, hiking, rocks, mud, swamps, or animals she left to the workers on her farm, or to me. But every now and then I insisted that we ride to a secluded spot—an island in the river or the dunes on the coast—and then I'd carry her the rest of the way. There also had to be accommodations: a blanket or chair on which to sit, a tent in case of bugs, a lantern to banish shadows, and extra shoes and clothes. Yet she was very game about it all. And I must admit it's a turn-on to see a perfectly dressed and coiffed woman standing at midnight amid the vines, dark trees, sloughs, snakes, and night birds.

not to get blood on the carpet or the sofa. And then he has to go. It's a little boring, but it's steady and bankable. This also tends to be an arrangement that thrives in the country, or in rural places, where the vampire can behave a bit more like a human husband—working in the driveway, or puttering around the garage—without many people seeing him.

**HOW YOU'LL GET ALONG:** As long as everything is "just fine," he'll eventually move in with you, in a lightproof master bedroom, so he'll have more time to get things done around the house. But sometimes the steadiness and repetitiveness will get to both of you, and he'll flip out and run off for a few weeks. Don't worry—he's just sulking about one mile away, alone, and hungry.

9. **QUESTING LOVERS:** Imagine a vampire who likes to watch "Survivor Man" and reads *Outside*, and a woman who's into the same, and who both want to travel around the world. I've done a bit of this myself: Strap on a really good backpack, or outfit a sailboat, and set off. Your vampire can obtain everything you need along the way, and you've got everything he needs. Plus, you're the kind of gal who turns him on— you're a rock climber, sailor, scuba diver, or back country skier. But you're going to have to be hard-core, because you're going to be moving at night, and when you're deep in rough

country, you're going to be eating whatever your vampire man can catch: fish, varmints, possibly a moose. To my knowledge, no vampire has ever summited K2 or Everest—we're usually too caught up in other things to mount a major expedition in a country riven with superstitions—but don't be surprised if one of us does eventually.

**HOW YOU'LL GET ALONG:** Either you're going with this guy and your life will be nomadic, exhilarating, and a bit starved for human interaction, or you're going to stick with the life you have, and he'll come back to you between quests (if you'll have him) to regale you with tales of avalanches and trigger-happy border guards.

10. **MYSTERIOUS WAYS:** This is the blood couple version of *Last Tango in Paris.* You meet, he feeds, you go at it like mad, and then you part. And you keep doing this, meeting after meeting. You make no mention of the facts and events of your lives, and neither of you seeks that information (the vampire, however, will know a few more scant details about you than you know about him). You have an intense, almost maddening attraction for each other, something that you know could totally upend your life and his if you tried for a full-fledged relationship. In fact, this intense, maddening attraction might be all there is to the two of you. You can't

figure it out, you don't want to, and you won't. But one day, one of you won't show up.

**HOW YOU'LL GET ALONG:** Dress to kill and just keep throwing yourselves at each other—it's going to burn up in a glorious ball of red flame.

# Compatibility Checklist—Are You the Right Couple?

Vampires keep everything about themselves recorded in their heads; they know what they did when, and they know what they liked. But

as checklists have become a staple of human self-assessment, we'll have several here, mostly for your use but also for discussion with your vampire.

First is a compatibility checklist, which can help you decide how much of a relationship you have going right now, and what sort of future it might have. There's one major thing to bear in mind: Vampires do change, but usually you can't change them forcibly. While you can ask a vampire to do things differently for the sake of your enjoyment, pleasure, or safety, this is a conscious and limited behavior change. What is fundamental to a vampire's being remains fundamental, unless something profound happens to him and shows him that his very nature will misguide him.

## About Him:

1. Is your vampire similar enough to the kind of vampire you hoped you would meet? Y___ N___ M___

2. Do you think that your vampire makes an effort to accommodate your human schedule and physiology? Y ___ N___ M___

3. Does he arrive at or close to the time he said he would? Y___ N___ M___

4. If you ask your vampire not to take too much blood, does he respond? Y___ N___ M___

5. Does your vampire carry on too forcefully, or does he stop when you tell him he's scaring you, hurting you, or causing you to black out? Y___ N___ M___

6. When you venture out in public, does he stay close to you and not slip away to feed randomly? Y___ N___ M___

7. If you are turned off by the odor of other people's blood on his breath, does he make sure to brush his teeth before arriving? Y___ N___ M___

8. Is he reasonable about your sexual limits? Y___ N___ M___

9. Is he open to your need to function as much like a human couple as possible? Y___ N___ M___

10. Does he respect you as a woman? Y___ N___ M___

11. Does he seem to be capable of getting serious; i.e., marrying you? Y___ N___ M___

12. Does he surprise you pleasantly, such as with gifts or sudden visits at proper times? Y___ N___ M___

13. If he belongs to a coven, does he seem honest about his coven activities when he does tell you about them? Y___ N___ M___

## About You:

1. Do you get turned on by the way he feeds from you? Y___ N___ M___

2. Are you a physical match for your vampire—do you have the energy, endurance, and sufficient blood? Y___ N___ M___

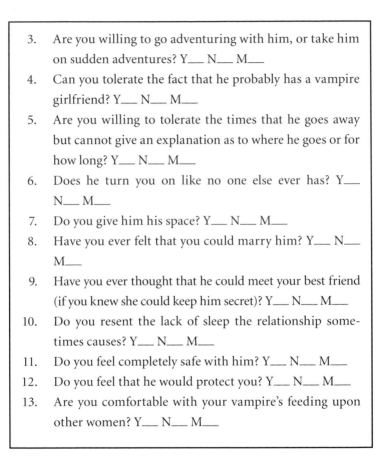

3. Are you willing to go adventuring with him, or take him on sudden adventures? Y\_\_ N\_\_ M\_\_

4. Can you tolerate the fact that he probably has a vampire girlfriend? Y\_\_ N\_\_ M\_\_

5. Are you willing to tolerate the times that he goes away but cannot give an explanation as to where he goes or for how long? Y\_\_ N\_\_ M\_\_

6. Does he turn you on like no one else ever has? Y\_\_ N\_\_ M\_\_

7. Do you give him his space? Y\_\_ N\_\_ M\_\_

8. Have you ever felt that you could marry him? Y\_\_ N\_\_ M\_\_

9. Have you ever thought that he could meet your best friend (if you knew she could keep him secret)? Y\_\_ N\_\_ M\_\_

10. Do you resent the lack of sleep the relationship sometimes causes? Y\_\_ N\_\_ M\_\_

11. Do you feel completely safe with him? Y\_\_ N\_\_ M\_\_

12. Do you feel that he would protect you? Y\_\_ N\_\_ M\_\_

13. Are you comfortable with your vampire's feeding upon other women? Y\_\_ N\_\_ M\_\_

If you answered "Yes" to eight or more of the questions in either checklist, you're doing all right. If you answered "No" or "Maybe" to five or more, you and your vampire have some work to do, relationship wise. You vampire might seem hard to get through to but that's not the case, exactly. Vampires are strange beasts, very set in their ways; much like men, they require a bit of influencing, even training or trickery, to bend to your wants and will. They'll respect you for it, actually, for unlike men, vampires don't mind a bit of subterfuge for the sake of a pleasurable result. A strong will enabled by cleverness and subtlety will impresses a vampire.

## Pleasure Checklist: Are You Having Enough Fun?

Now, let us consider a checklist that is much more appealing: making sure you're getting what you want, and him, too. You could make a game of it, reading the questions to each other, and eliminating "No" answers on the spot:

---

### For You:
1. Does feeding arouse you as part of foreplay? Y___ N___ M___
2. Does your vampire kiss nicely, without fang interference? Y___ N___ M___
3. Do you get aroused when he says hot, sexy things about drinking your blood? Y___ N___ M___
4. Is it thrilling when you let him physically dominate you? Y___ N___ M___

---

5.  Does his physical potency as a vampire make you more orgasmic? Y___ N___ M___

6.  Do you like to be fed upon before and/or during orgasm? Y___ N___ M___

7.  Do you find yourself feeling more sexually free with a vampire partner? Y___ N___ M___

8.  Do you find that you are able to indulge specific fantasies because of the natural kinkiness of vampires? Y___ N___ M___

9.  Do you feel more sexually complete when your vampire performs romantic or erotic rituals than you've felt with human partners? Y___ N___ M___

10. Do you feel free to initiate sexual activity regardless of what your vampire is doing (talking, feeding, bathing)? Y___ N___ M___

11. Do you dress in ways that you have never dressed before to provoke his sexual response? Y___ N___ M___

12. Do most of your role-playing games or fantasies hinge entirely on his being a vampire or drinking your blood? Y___ N___ M___

13. Does he touch you in sexually pleasurable ways while feeding from you? Y___ N___ M___

14. Does watching him feed upon another woman arouse you? Y___ N___ M___

Maybe half a dozen times in my life, a woman created a daytime refuge for me in her home. In every case, the house was very large, allowing me to select a room that simply could be written off as "storage" and create my daybed there. This occurred only after many months of our being involved, and only under my own specifications. Vampires frequently encounter girlfriends who wish for their lover to stay through a day with them, into the next night, or do so for several days and nights. This is a very nice, romantic idea, but a vampire cannot spend extended amounts of time in your home unless, somehow, a very secure resting place is created for him; a place where no one—none of your friends, nor any building inspectors, utility workers, or nosy neighbors—will ever venture. So do not be hurt if your vampire is leery about an extended stay. Such a fun thing can be had if, in fact, you can be assured of a good deal of seclusion, and seclusion can be found in many places, in the city and in the country.

15. Do you fantasize about being with other vampires while he makes love to you? Y___ N___ M___

## For Him:

1. Does he drink enough of your blood to fulfill his sexual attraction to you? Y___ N___ M___

2. Is he satisfied with the duration of lovemaking and feeding? Y___ N___ M___

3. Does he enjoy making you climax when he isn't actively feeding? Y___ N___ M___

4. Is he able to climax without drinking your blood? Y___ N___ M___

5. Is he willing to engage in sexual activity outdoors or in locations that are not perfectly secure? Y___ N___ M___

6. Does he happily indulge role-playing games that you suggest, even those that put you in a dominant role over him? Y___ N___ M___

7. Does he awake from his sleep aroused by thoughts of you? Y___ N___ M___

8. Is he often ready to try different activities that you suggest, even if these delay his feeding? Y___ N___ M___

9. Does he spend entire nights with you when he can? Y___ N___ M___

10. Does he ask for the two of you to perform specific activities or acts, aside from feeding, that he specifically enjoys? Y__ N__ M__

11. Does he still enjoy courting you for your blood? Y__ N__ M__

12. Does he use blood courtship as a part of foreplay? Y__ N__ M__

13. Does he fantasize about you being fed upon by other vampires? Y__ N__ M__

14. Does he attempt to prolong sex or delay orgasm by quickly feeding from you before he climaxes? Y__ N__ M__

15. Does he encourage having a third partner if he is allowed to choose the woman? Y__ N__ M__

While neither of you will answer "Yes" to every question above, I would hope that you answer thus to most of the questions, including those most applicable to the particular nature of your romance. There is so much to consider in *l'affaire vampire* that trying to monitor or consider all of it at once is not so easy. There are many compromises to be made—first and foremost the compromises your starkly different natures will require of your lives—but they are specific and limited, and are made so that your overall sexual and personal pleasure is supreme.

While I've usually been very well behaved with the women in my life, I once did make a woman extremely angry; in the summer of 1946, while I was showing a newly arrived vampire around New York City. I was dressed as a returning naval officer, and my charge, a pretty Polish émigré, was dressed as a Navy nurse, costumes that lent themselves to our going largely unnoticed as we skirted the edges of USO mixers while I showed this female vampire how to navigate an American social crowd. While dancing with her in a somewhat dark ballroom, I happened to look to my right and see none other than the woman I had left behind in the city, Miranda, when I had departed for the aforementioned operation on the Eastern Front. She was obviously overwhelmed by seeing me, but she also recognized that at the moment I was undercover, so to speak, so she continued to dance with an Army officer who yanked her around the dance floor like a sack. When the song was over, my woman and I met outside, where she popped me flush on the jaw a lot harder than I ever would have guessed she could, but then she wrapped her arms around me and cried. I hadn't told her I was back in the country, as my duties weren't yet complete, and writing to each other was nearly impossible while I was gone. Worried I was dead, she had gone out with a bunch of girlfriends to find new "fellas," human ones. I also had a lot of explaining to do about the "nurse" with me, and that only made matters worse. But, eventually, I got back together with Miranda, when all my duties were dispensed, and I once again took off the uniform of my country and slipped back into the comfort of legendary anonymity.

## Measuring Your Reactions— A Situational Test

As we shall get into some sections about troubleshooting in your vampiric relationship, you might take this quick test below just to gauge your anticipatory reactions to some of those things that can occur in a romance with a vampire. These things in and of themselves are not things that could or should necessarily end your romance, but they will make for a strange and indelicate moment. Such peccadilloes go with the territory; we vampires are an impulsive, instinctive, libidinal, grandiose, and sensationalistic lot. Sometimes, as they say, we "slip up."

Rate these situations on a scale of one to six, one being in complete agreement, two being open-minded, with some reservations, three being mildly disconcerted but open to discussion, four being strong dislike, five being outrage, and six being the deal breaker.

1.  Your vampire's fangs hurt a bit too much, and you find that you're more comfortable when he uses a dagger. But he says he must use his fangs sometimes to enjoy feeding from you fully.

2.  Your vampire often asks you to meet him on his own turf, or in remote locations. You find often find these locations to be unromantic, but he insists on them as a security measure.

3.  You can never get your vampire to give you a specific time that he will arrive at your home—he can only agree, in advance, to the particular date. The few times you asked him to please arrive by midnight, he didn't show until three AM, and he doesn't seem willing to change.

4.  That's not a bloodstain on his shirt collar—it's lipstick. But he offers a very straightforward answer: "She fainted right after I fed from her—just did a face plant right into me."

5.   Your vampire spies on you when you're out with your girl-friends (who don't know you're seeing him), and then, one by one, he hypnotizes and feeds from them. He's the one who tells you this and says he did not sleep with them, but confesses, "I wanted to know what they taste like. They won't remember, and if they do, they won't say anything."

6.   Your vampire mentions that he has had a vampire girl-friend for a number of years and that she has met his human lovers on occasion. When you ask if he is currently seeing her, he says, "Yes. But it's completely different from our relationship and shouldn't mean anything to you."

7.   You have a twin sister, and your vampire insists that he be allowed to at least feed from her. You feel a lot of pres-sure to agree but know that you won't.

8.   You've only discussed a threesome when your vampire boyfriend shows up one night with another woman who has willingly come along. Your vampire expects you to jump right in.

9.   Several of your vampire's covenmates are bringing their human girlfriends to a spring equinox party at the coven house, where the girlfriends will give blood upon the vampire altar. He wants you to do the same, and allow members of the coven to feed from you. "They will feed from your wrist, and I will stop it before you've lost any real quantity of blood," he says.

10. Your vampire insists that he be the only male—human or vampire—in your life while you're together. You wish you could manage this, but you've had a long-time, on-again, off-again human boyfriend. Your vampire discovers this and demands that you dump the boyfriend or he, the vampire, will scare him off.

11. After half a dozen months of the most enjoyable romance you've ever known, your vampire says he might have to do some traveling soon. The next you hear from him, it's in a letter, and he says he will be gone a long time. You don't hear from him for six months. But then one night he returns, expecting to pick up where you left off. "I cannot tell you where I went or what I did," he says, "and this new vampire you're seeing is a punk—please get rid of him or I will."

12. You lose your job, and your vampire invites you on a long vacation. You want to go, but you're worried about losing your home. The next day, your vampire tells you that he came into a great deal of cash—enough for a year of mortgage payments—and wants to write you a check, but he won't tell where the money came from.

If you answer up to nine questions with a one, two, or three, you clearly have a bit of a wild streak, and are probably having the time of your life, too. But remember that women who stand up to vampires impress them, so don't take at face value everything he says, asks for, or does. Assert yourself.

If you answer upwards of six to eight questions with a four or a five, you clearly have some troubles with the more extreme or transgressive behavior of a vampire boyfriend. While such behavior is not a constant, when it happens, you're going to have a difficult time sorting it out. Your best bet is to address these sorts of romantic or libidinal misdemeanors early in the relationship, set your margins of tolerance, and hold to them. Of course, you can always dump one fanged man for another of greater refinement or self-control.

If you answer up to four questions with a six, then you have a problem, because there's always a chance that even the most constant vampire lover will give in to an impulse or long-ignored indulgence, or turn his attention to some business related to his coven or vampire associations that will wholly absorb him, and for which he can offer little apology or explanation. If up to a third of what you encountered in the survey is utterly intolerable, you have just a few options: Change your own point of view. Ignore your dislike. Avoid vampires entirely.

You didn't expect a perfect world, did you?

# 7

# Once He Has Your Heart

That was a tricky chapter, full of questions and hard answers, wasn't it? But you've gotten through it—you know your limits, the nature of your relationship with your vampire, and the sexual needs and deeds that most delight you both. Now you must consider those things that are factors of a continuing relationship with your man of night, those things that add up after a while and change you, sometimes subtracting from you, other times or in other ways adding to your life greatly. The maintenance aspects of a relationship with a vampire can shape and define it as much as the sexual aspects.

## Enduring the Times Apart

As noted earlier, your vampire might, at times, have to depart for places unknown to you, for reasons he cannot speak. More than likely, this has to do with vampire associations that require his

The greatest amount I was ever able to drink from a lover in one night without her losing consciousness was one-and-a-half pints. That's a lot for most size eights, which was the average body size at that time. But such blood drinking was not done all in one shot, and my girlfriend drank water and ate some food over the course of the evening. With other women, two complete mouthfuls were all they could surrender before they began to feel light-headed, or get a headache. You and your boyfriend are going to have to figure out your maximum bloodletting very carefully, through a little trial and error. For good blood health, get proper quantities of protein and sufficient amounts of iron, from either vegetable or animal sources (spinach, apples, fish, and good steaks rank high); hit your full USDA recommendations at least four times a week. After that, drink water. No, you don't have to be one of those people who doesn't go anywhere without a quart of designer-label bottled water. But blood is mostly water, and blood loss leads to dehydration. Beyond that, you should get a decent supply of complex carbohydrates and leafy green vegetables, and orange and red vegetables. These add certain flavors to your blood. Shortly before you know you're going to be fed upon, try eating something sweet, or a combination of spices. These can flavor your blood in enjoyable ways. You and your vampire can experiment. In the past, I have enjoyed combinations of saffron, ginger, and coconut. Sweet fruits such as apples, pears, and pineapple have put a bouquet on many a blood meal I've enjoyed with a considerate lady. Whiskeys, dark rum, and strong red wines add a nice muskiness, but alcohol dehydrates you, so take heed.

direct help, or observation. Sometimes this amounts to nothing more than what might be considered a weekend's business trip.

But if you learn that he must go away for an extended time, you should plan for a romantic night together before his departure, thus

giving yourself the opportunity to ask for his pledge of faithfulness
and intention to return to you.

His pledge will be in two steps. First, he will make a shallow
cut in his wrist, drawing blood into a tiny pool, and then do the
same to you. He will then spill droplets of your blood into his, and
then drink this mixture off his skin, and state, "Your blood is in
my blood, and my blood is of your blood—both return me to
you," or words to that effect, as some pledges use archaic or foreign
languages. The second step is that he will give you something very
important to him, a personal object that symbolizes his need to
return to you. This is often a piece of his jewelry, or possibly an
heirloom of his human life. While this item is of great material and
personal value to him, the fact that you hold it is the importance that
it highlights. In effect, you hold, literally, pieces of your vampire's
life and are a giver of life, and he will come back to you.

He will stay with you as long as he can the night before his
departure. But then he most likely will need a full day's rest, and at
the very next sunset, he will set off.

What do you do while he is gone?

As everyone has experienced in the absence of a lover, there
is a return to the individualized schedule. You'll start doing those
things you like to do for yourself for which you haven't had the
time, lately, between job, personal or family life, and vampire.

But there is one thing that exists these days that never did before: the ability for a woman to use the Internet to reach out to other women who are in the same predicament. While in the past, pairs or very small groups of women who loved vampires were able to unite using carefully worded or coded classified ads, the digital age affords much more extensive outreach of a much greater variety. There are numerous, all-women societies—I wouldn't call them "support groups," as they are much more than that—that give a vampire-loving woman a refuge, some that actually meet, and some that exist wholly on-line.

The thing to be careful about with such groups is the fact that vampire hunters can penetrate them. Acceptance to such a group, therefore, is not a quick and ready process. And this is why, more often than not, women who have such a sisterhood do so in very small, localized numbers; these are women who have probably seen each other in social situations, or around town, and develop a hunch about the other.

What if you're not a "joiner"? You'd rather eke this out on your own, right?

You'll do fine. Those people who prefer their own company when not in the company of someone they love tend to be highly adaptive people. They pick up something where they left off—a long book, a painting, an instrument, a family history, a quilt. Don't let that sound quaint to you. Great artists often work alone, at least in their heads.

As for other coping methods for dealing with your vampire's absence, there are these:

1. **MEDITATION AND POSITIVE VISUALIZATION:** When you know you'll be stressed by his being away, set aside some time for meditation or quiet concentration. Picture the things you want to do that you'll enjoy while he's gone. Picture him being out of harm's way, and of being successful. Picture the day that he returns.

2. **TAKE A VACATION:** Hey, if he's going away, so are you—but your trip is going to be fun (whereas his is vampire business) and will give you unlimited personal time. Go with some girlfriends, or go to a place where you can stay with some friends, or go alone. Women do need to learn to travel alone more—you never know what can happen when you're wholly unencumbered.

3. **RECONNECT WITH FRIENDS, OR DEVELOP A NEW SOCIAL GROUP:** You always wanted to join the bowling league, but their night games put a crimp in your plans with the boyfriend? Now's the chance to get on the lanes. Friends who had a tendency to indulge late-night dinners will be surprised by your call. Take along a nice bottle of red.

4.   **THE TEMPORARY STAND-IN:** Admit it—you thought of this as soon as your vampire said he'd be out of the country for a month. You're not going to sleep with this guy and you know you're not going to fall for him. But he's single, and cute (and human), and you know where he lives, and you know you would both enjoy the companionship. If he gets interested, just tell him you're on hiatus from a major relationship but plan on getting back together. If he (ineptly) views that as his cue to pull you into his camp, let him pay for everything and then disappoint him terribly—he'll get the message that this is a purely social effort.

Warfare and soldiering are familiar to vampires, usually in resistance to vampire hunters, and sometimes in coven-to-coven conflicts. Military wives and girlfriends are most used to a spouse or boyfriend spending long periods away, and they know best how to deal with it directly. The trouble for the girlfriend of the vampire is that she cannot so readily form those social and support groups that military wives can. But there are a number of underground associations, comprised of the girlfriends of vampires, that form up when those women must endure a long absence. How do you find one? Most of these groups have an active representative who will flash a group symbol or icon in certain venues—certain bars, neighborhoods, or private gatherings—similar to the way a Mason wears a Masonic ring or chain. Given what you have seen of vampiric graffiti, you will notice this image, and it will register. Another way is to find out from your vampire before he leaves if there are any other girlfriends of his covenmates who have such an association. More than likely they do. The question for you is do you want to become that much more involved with coven-connected people, or do you prefer an independent situation with your boyfriend?

# Dealing with Jealousy

As your relationship evolves over time, you will come to realize that your vampire must have fed from other women numerous times. This, as stated, is nothing that you can worry about—he gets his nutrition where he can, and if he has given his word that he has no other involvements with human women, you can only take him at his word.

But when you're involved with a sort of man who could very easily have any woman he wanted, you're going to have to sort out your emotions about that, for really you are jealous of the *potential* for another woman to come into his orbit. I can tell you from experience that sometimes a woman nearly psyches herself out with jealous worry that is just wasted energy. Presented with the face and voice of jealousy, a vampire is usually a bit put off by this wrinkle in your trust, and given to a mirthful disregard for these emotions.

Belonging to the woman who loves a vampire is the necessity of bearing up under the emotions inherent to involvement with such a strange humanoid creature. And jealousy being the opposite of lust, it can craze you.

You must create a kind of mental and emotional demarcation and live within those margins, but that doesn't mean you can't live fully. That is to say, that when your vampire is with you—when he comes to you, swoons over you, tastes your blood, makes love to you, and protects you—he is all yours and you all his. To enjoy this even more you must trust him, as trust gives the go-ahead for full emotional expression of your amorous feelings.

But what if you know that there is, somewhere out there, a vampire who is your man's otherworldly girlfriend? How do you deal with that fact without pulling out your hair?

You must first talk to your vampire boyfriend about her, and find out if he is even in contact with her. Remember what I said earlier—once young vampires understand their functional immortality, they realize they can form bonds that span centuries. There is, thus, the possibility that in the last five years, he has not seen this vampire woman, and does not know if he will see her in the next five years.

So perhaps what makes you jealous is the fact that his vampire-to-vampire relationship can span so many more years than yours can. But once you start letting your mortality and faster aging arouse your jealousy, you are, in fact, in contest with the whole human condition. You will get nowhere with this.

You might fear, however, that after some time together, your vampire man will somehow find his way toward that distant female vampire, and that this could upset or end your life together. You can only attempt to clarify this beforehand, and get your man's promise that he either put aside his vampiric love while he is with you, or you will have to be separated if he goes to her for any length of time, and there is no way of knowing if you would get back together. That seems like an ultimatum, but you have to fight for what you need on the most crucial subjects.

# Setting Your Personal and Romantic Standards

In a sense, what I tried to clarify with the section above is what your personal limits are: what you will tolerate from your vampire. No woman wants to be the one to whom either a man or vampire "returns" after he has dallied with someone who has sway over him. As a woman once put it to me so eloquently, "I will not allow you to run off every three or four years to vacation with your fanged girl knowing that there will be that one time when I wait for you to return and you don't, because I will be too old. If you leave me once, you must leave me for good."

I couldn't ignore that. So I didn't.

It all depends on what you're looking for from your vampire and in your vampiric relationship. A number of women I've known did tolerate the fact that I had a long-standing connection with a female vampire; some of them tolerated this quite easily, because they understood both the nature of being a vampire and sympathized with its strange dualities.

Every woman has a good friend or sibling who is also the nosiest person in the world. Nosiness is a combination of envy and subterfuge: The nosy person needs to know about you so she can compare herself and see how you both rate, with the intention of advancing herself using the information that she gains. Once, my girlfriend in Texas had an almost-best friend who would turn up on short notice at my girlfriend's house on such a frequent basis, I began to suspect her of some ulterior motive (an antivampire connection?) because this woman always knew when my girlfriend was home. But good womanly, Texas manners prevented my love from immediately shooing this woman away, and

This is, in a sense, what it means for the human lover of a vampire to become vampirelike in her approach to romance. The lifelong monogamy demanded by the cultural, personal, and societal mores of humans who seek an idealized but wholly limited sexual and romantic experience are sorely tested by a vampire's nature. We cleave to the human women we love as intensely and this began to cut into our quality time. How do you effectively handle Miss Nosy while involved with a vampire? You have to fabricate some sort of social crisis as a distraction, something that will draw her away from you entirely. Tell her that you have good information that her position on the museum board is in jeopardy if she doesn't increase her volunteer hours. Or her reign as director of the garden society could soon come to an end if she doesn't stop her husband from chasing the mayor's daughter. Nosy people deserve a smoke screen. Terrifically nosy people deserve deception—it's what they're asking for.

thoroughly as we can. And this is what it means for a vampire to return to something of his humanity in romance with you.

## Dealing with Human Suspicions

As the old adage goes, "When love blooms, worry less about your vampire and more about your friends." For not very many people who know you will get along completely with the changes in lifestyle and personal hours that come along in this kind of love life.

A great deal depends, however, on how you conduct your social life. If you're one of those people who can disappear for a while, only to reappear later and have everyone ask, "Hey, where've you been?" but still like you, then you should be fine. But as things go these days, you're probably enmeshed in a wide social network that you very much need and want to be a part of, to say nothing of the job contacts. How do you manage?

First, enlist your vampire's help. He'll understand your predicament. Figure out ways that you can both be most flexible in your meetings when such flexibility is a necessity. While a vampire can have his strong feelings about you, he's well aware that the stability of your social and family life is crucial to the camouflage of your romance. The suspicious father or brother-in-law can easily become the vampire-hunter informant if his suspicions are too greatly aroused. Your vampire would take great pleasure in seeing you every night, but he knows that this is impractical for both of you.

Second, pick your parties. While some events, such as your sister's engagement party, are musts, you can make an executive decision now and then about where to go and what to do. The key is to put in enough of an appearance at the right time in the best scene. You might make more of a splash at a loft party where you don't know that many people, but a quiet evening at a low-key bar with several very close friends might be more important in the long run if you need to solidify a friendship at that gathering.

Three, effectively manage people. Sure, a synonym for this might be *manipulation*, but as they say at your office, "Everyone is a manager now." And the way to manage people vis-à-vis your vampiric affair is to control what they know and when they see you. Give them as much of yourself as you can, otherwise—when they need help or advice, or someone to talk to—be as selective as need be about yourself. If people question this directly, just ask their forgiveness and chalk it up to your attempts to keep a very busy life under control, and quickly apply the fourth item, below.

Four, always have an effective cover story. Ah, how to do this without lying outright. If you work in public relations, it will be a cinch. Just always deliver a basic story that is highly plausible and one that's easy to remember. The trouble comes when people press for details about these explanations. Go easy on the fine details, and give the most basic sketch you can. Indeed, this is, to a degree, actual lying, but then again there are few people who have an actual right to know the details of your personal life, and even those people you must mislead just a bit.

## Protecting Your Vampire

Now that you have an established relationship, your responsibilities to your vampire will become clear. And that relationship itself, having become an ongoing effort, with a history and a structure, is something that you will have to help conceal. You will also have to conceal your vampire man. Powerful as he is, your boyfriend's life is very much in your hands. He is willing to expose himself to a degree to love you, but you must do your best to limit any exposure that you could cause inadvertently. There are a number of requirements on this count

## Do You Tell Anyone?

Some people have trouble with big secrets. They begin to implode under their weight, and the existence of such an important person in your life is something that is very difficult to keep under wraps, especially if you are stressed about certain aspects of the relationship, or have concerns about the future. You might also have one other person—a very close friend or a sister—to whom you can confide everything.

But that is a risky practice for you now, for several reasons. First of all, your greatest confidant might not understand your attraction to a vampire, and might, in fact, think this the height of dangerous romantic folly and insist that you end the affair immediately. Now you have made an adversary of your formerly most closely held friend. Secondly, you will have divulged information on which your vampire's life might hinge. If your friend or sister disapproves so mightily, and also, in fact, harbors the notion that she knows better for you than you do yourself, she might decide to take action. She might try to prevent you from meeting your vampire, or she might actually refuse to leave you alone, to the point of restraining you so that you remain in her presence. Worse, she could wait until she knows you must be meeting him, and then locate you with the vampire hunters at her heels.

Another problem you face in telling someone about your romance is that he or she simply won't understand, as alluded to above. The person might not oppose it outright, but there will be a large gap in your empathies, and this can only cause friction.

Finally, you don't know if this person can keep a secret of this magnitude because you've never before told a big secret (or have you?). Your usual confidant might take this as an astounding and even shocking revelation, one that surpasses her usual discretion and surety.

There are, perhaps, just two conditions under which you could tell a confidant about your romance. The first, as discussed before, is with a woman who is also involved with a vampire now, or has been in the past. But given that such a person will most likely be a stranger to you upon meeting, you will have to maintain as much anonymity as you can until you know for a fact this woman belongs to the same sisterhood. The second situation is one in which you have told a close, trustworthy friend of your interest in vampires and your intention to pursue a romance before actually meeting a vampire. Knowing your inclinations beforehand and being wholly sympathetic might enable this person to live up to the level of secrecy needed. This person might have his or her own interest in vampires, and while that can be a boon, you must also be careful this person's interest does not become a liability or attempt to match yours.

At the end of the day, I might be inclined to tell you that the best mantra about your romance is, "Tell no one, tell no one, tell no one." But there is one distinct advantage to having a close friend who knows of your romance and can keep it quiet: This person can help in ways that the uninformed cannot. She, or he, can help with occasional cover stories, providing corroboration, or help you with direct issues, such as sun proofing a bedroom, or getting a crucial message to your vampire when you cannot.

These people are few and cannot often promise their support over significant periods of time. If you do have or find one, treat her well and kindly, and give back to her the same extensive support, but always know that you will withhold much more information than you divulge.

## Deniability

If suddenly one day the police, FBI, or a horribly nosy neighbor bursts in your door and says, "We know you're involved with a vampire—you cannot deny it," how could you deny it successfully? Because you can forget about any kind of daredevil reaction in which you claim to love, love, *love* vampires, declaring that you are deeply and passionately involved with one whose name is Luc Richard and he lives somewhere on the East Coast. Please don't do something like that—it will just lead to a lot of trouble. Some people still remember the Communist witch hunts of the 1950s, but fewer are aware anymore of the Massachusetts witch hunts of the late 1600s (witchcraft was actually classified as a *felony* then). But there will be continual efforts much like this, conducted by "authorities" of all types, who wish to root out those women who tend to love what such authorities believe is a deviancy, and will either attempt to "cure" those women, imprison them, or exile them. The real goal of such efforts, however, is to detect and exterminate us vampires.

So, how do you declaim accusations of a vampiric romance? Deniability hinges on the total lack of any witnesses or evidence that would indicate the presence of a vampire in your life—any substantive material that investigators could obtain, illegally or with a warrant, such as photos, blood evidence, letters, daggers, and, of course, any marks on you.

That latter item is crucial to your vampire's need to bite or stab carefully and selectively, and allow bite or stab sites to heal. But what about the rest—all the trappings of romance that you would hope you could enjoy and indulge without a care?

All material things—photos, letters, jewelry, or other vampire items, such as daggers—will have to be carefully hidden. You might even conceal them away from your premises, if you think it wise. No one wants to censor themselves in a love letter, so you can't be expected to make no reference to vampiric things in your missals to one another. Writing in code is also obvious. So, if you have a cache of love letters, and also photos, hide them as best you can, and be ready to burn them, if need be, terrible as that sounds. Don't keep any digital photos on your computer or phone, if you can help it.

Blood evidence is a bit trickier. Of course, the only traces of blood in your home will be your own, and this is a perfectly natural thing given that most accidents occur in the home. But be sure to clean up any places where a significant quantity of your blood either spilled or stained some material. Always wash any glasses or other containers that might have held your blood soon after your vampire leaves, as more than one woman has been caught because she kept, for sentimental reasons, a cordial glass that had once contained her blood. "But why," the chief of detectives says, "would you fill a glass with your own blood?" That's a difficult question to answer.

As for deniability about the time you spend with your vampire, you're the only person who knows where you were when you were alone with your vampire, unless you do indeed have an intimate friend who helps you on occasion, and who knows about your boyfriend. But when it's just you and your vampire alone, you can always say you spent the evening by yourself. The cops will be hard put to place a vampire in your midst.

Yes, deniability becomes a problem if you ever confide to a close friend your great, secret amour, or if you also have this person help on occasion, by providing an empty house, or cover story. You've no control over what this person thinks or says. And when the heat is on, you can never know if your friend will have her own airtight alibi, or will cave.

No woman truly in love ever wants to deny her lover or what she feels for him. But in this case, deniability is tantamount to saving his life.

Is making such denials to law enforcement illegal? Well, lying to a cop or a Fed *is* illegal, but as of yet, being involved with a vampire does not break any specific statutes that I'm aware of, given that there's nothing (yet) on the books about vampires specifically, though I'm sure there's some "unnatural relations" catchall category. But because law enforcement is loathe to reveal what it knows about vampires or what it is investigating about us—in fact, it's all quite secret—any accusations about your dalliances would never arrive in open court. So you're basically caught up in a secret persecution, something that runs counter to the stated methods of enforcing the law and upholding justice. This, unfortunately, has become a standard in a post 9/11 world. You have a right to resist that.

## Resisting Antivampire Factions

Groups that work to detect, root out, hunt, and destroy vampires are widespread, but not always well organized, and they are rather secretive. They are sometimes smaller units of large "philanthropic" organizations; ad hoc groups of private citizens, city council members, and business leaders; or actual state security or state contracted paramilitary units. I was once even chased by a bunch of U.S. Postal Service workers.

Unfortunately, these reactionaries often function along the same patterns as you do in seeking a vampire amore—by going to

I could always count on my Washington, D.C. girl-friend back in the early 1960s to throw curve balls at the most dogged antivampire hunters—those from the FBI's Section 59, which investigated matters of the occult (J. Edgar Hoover was fascinated by vampirism but refused to believe it was anything more than human cult activity). Twice I was followed on my way to her home, and both times I eluded my pursuers and found my way to her back door. But much to my chagrin, the FBI agents that had glimpsed me somehow pegged Vanessa's home, and went there twice to interview her. She first put them in touch with a respected Catholic priest who vouched for her presence at a regular midnight mass, and the second time asked them to contact a Republican senator's son with whom she had a standing date every Thursday. I had no idea she had these contingencies in place, and they were enough to mollify the spooks for a short time. After that, I adopted a wholly new protocol for our dates, and kept the FBI off our backs.

those places that vampires might frequent, and by spying on people, often women, who are regularly active at night. They will sometimes even impersonate vampires or women who seek vampires for the sake of entrapment. But there are ways to resist their schemes:

1. Study closely your vampire's eyes upon meeting. No one has yet been able to fake the blood-tinged pleura of a vampire's eyes. A contact lens that attempts to mimic this will not appear natural. Bloodshot eyes don't count, and are an easy giveaway.

2. Be careful of women whom you don't know, who ask questions that lead to questions about vampires. Now, such a gal might very well be on the same quest as you. And in that case, she's the local competition. If she's an undercover vampire hunter, she's a competitor of the worst kind. But indulge the conversation—don't hastily change the subject. You might learn something. Ultimately, give up no concrete information, and remember this woman's face.

3. When you are in a vampire romance, be very careful of strangers whom you let into your home, especially utility service people. Always be sure to have an actual

appointment with your cable, electric, or water service, and obtain beforehand the ID number of the service person who's been dispatched so you can check it when he or she arrives. If antivampire forces have tagged you as someone who has a vampire boyfriend, they might want to set up surveillance equipment in your home. That's illegal, of course, but they don't care, because this isn't about justice for them.

4.  If you and your vampire enjoy occasional courtship in public places, albeit those places for nocturnal humans where you and he will blend right in, be wary of people too eager to get to know you. This might simply be a come-on by an attracted party, or it might be an investigator playing a hunch. In either case, trust your gut and your vampire's senses.

None of this is written to scare you off romance. But you must be aware that beyond your family and friends, there are those people who don't want your vampire romance to happen. It is to their eyes a deviancy that could lead to a breakdown in the moral order to which they would force everyone to ascribe. I can't blame humans for destroying dangerous vampires that kill people. They make no exception, unfortunately, for the more peaceable vampires who become involved with human partners, or those that carefully manage the blood.

## Troubleshooting Issues in Your Romance

One thing to keep in mind about vampires is that we were once men, so we still contain within us something of the nature of men, those beasts which you surely know are far from perfect and at times entirely useless. And then there are the most basic elements of our vampire nature, which can possibly be described as animal level instincts for survival and self-preservation. All of which is to say that vampires sometimes make what can only be described as mistakes within the context of their relationships with women. Some vampires would consider mistakes only those things that reveal their existence, identity, and location, or inhibited the obtaining of blood. Those are

probably not the vampires with whom you could have a productive romance.

But even in a romance, a vampire can do those things that obviously bother or freak you out. Impulse, thirst, and libido take us all into spaces we shouldn't enter. And you, too, will have your own liabilities, unto yourself, your relationship, and your vampire.

What follows is a partial list of those troubles, how to identify them, and how you can remedy them. Take them in stride. They're the occasional romantic hazards.

## Preying upon Your Friends

This is similar to the human boyfriend who can't keep himself from hitting on your friends, or even sleeping with them. In your vampire's case, however, he will have seen you with your friends sometime (the "spying on you issue" won't have been resolved) and picked one he found attractive. She might or might not have an attraction to vampires, and he might do his best to win her interest and willing submission. Why? Because having two lovely women willing to give him their blood and themselves appeals to him, despite the fact that he has much stronger feelings for you.

You will most likely find this out from your friend, as she will either be unable to keep the secret for long or will nearly become a doppelganger in her habits and attitudes. Once you've been involved with a vampire for a while, you'll develop a sixth sense about marking other women who are doing the same.

Should you tolerate this? Of course not. You will have to lay down the law with your vampire, and demand that he stop. On top of that, you have your few but crucial controls: You can declare that you will never give him your blood again; if he drinks it, he must take it. You will make your blood unsweet. You declare that you take no pleasure in his body, and renounce his protection. If these declarations don't hurt him they will at least insult him. Few gallant vampires will wish to perceive themselves as less than so, but insults that have merit reduce a vampire's sense of honor. A short time of going without your scent, the feel of your body as he feeds, and the taste of your blood—those things that affect him on his most sensual levels—will correct him.

## Going beyond Your Limits

Vampire-loving women come from all walks of life. And while a good number are not only ready for some high adventure but also have the lifestyle and means to indulge it, many of you have jobs, personal lives, and a future to build. So what are you supposed to do when your vampire wants to run off to Baja for three months and insists you come along? Or what if your vampire decides the time has come for you to meet some of his covenmates, and you suddenly find yourself in frequent, all-night revelries that leave you asleep at your desk at work? Then there's the sexual adventurousness of your blood-loving boyfriend—did you really expect to install a swing in your bedroom?

You must boldly and directly address all of these things with your vampire, and set your limits, for the sake of your livelihood and health. Any decent fellow who drinks your blood will understand; he knows what sort of extraordinary creature he is, in comparison to the human body and current habit of human work and living.

But you cannot disappoint him purposefully, and you cannot turn down too many of his far-flung ideas. There will have to be those times when you smash your routine, because doing so is healthy and routines that get old deserve to be smashed, or at least breached temporarily. Consider a few examples:

1. You've saved up three weeks of vacation time, two of which you intend to use visiting family. Your vampire has other ideas: a three week jaunt down the coast in a rented yacht, stopping at various hot spots along the way. You promise you can give him one week at the beach. He's willing to compromise, but he insists on accompanying you during your family visits, even

staying secretly in your auntie's or cousin's house, and he wants you to find him a secure resting place. Is that a workable compromise?

2. After a year of steady, monogamous involvement, your vampire invites you to a blood wedding at his coven, where a covenmate is marrying his human fiancée. You very much wish to go, in large part because you want his coven to see you and realize the depth of your love for one of their own, but you know that the wedding is traditional, meaning that the chief of the coven and the bride and groom taste the blood of every human guest. This will be done, as noted before, by a stab or bite on the wrist, but you are uncomfortable with other vampires feeding from you. Your vampire understands, and says you don't have to go, but he still plans to attend, and will take a vampire friend as his date. Is that OK with you?

3. Your vampire goes through distinctly horny phases every month (you think it has something to do with the gravitation effect of the moon), and one week out of the month, he wants to spend the entire night with

> you, sunup to sundown, in the throes of passion, hour after hour (feeding carefully but boffing excessively). You're exhausted by day three, and the second time this begins to happen, you have to call a time-out. When your boyfriend says this passion arises purely from his attraction to you and does not know what else to do, you realize he might be tempted to expend his libido elsewhere. How do you rise to the occasion?

Everyone has to set their own limits. Yes, routines should be broken, because they can become a rut. But you must quickly determine those things that you cannot bring yourself to do, or those things that you attempt and fail repeatedly, and find ways to live within your personal and sensuous means while still creating a fun and full romance with your vampire. As long as he sees that you are always taking yourself up to your limit, he will most often understand. He knows you're human; you both share in various frailties.

## Blood Idolatry

I've said before that you and your blood—your combined ability to emotionally and physically sustain us—are inseparable from our love for you. And we might play with your blood a bit like lovers use various foods in the bedroom.

Some vampires, however, can suffer from a disorder of emotions that is called blood idolatry. If you have noticed that over time your vampire pays much more interest in your blood itself, and in drawing it, looking at it, savoring it, and even talking about it the way a wine snob might overindulge his liking of a certain bottle. Some blood idolaters enjoy drawing their girlfriend's blood into a clear crystal chalice and drink it very slowly, admiring it, even saving it in a vial.

This misbehavior can take other forms. A vampire might carry with him a piece of plain cloth stained with his girlfriend's blood so that he can smell and taste it at will—doing so purely out of liking of the blood itself, not necessarily for the sake of thinking of the woman, as mentioned before. A blood idolater is more likely to have several human girlfriends, all for the sake of drawing a variety of blood that he can put into sample vials. A vampire who, like a laboratory technician, takes actual samples of your blood in collection tubes is most likely doing so to mix samples of human blood to create different tastes. In an uncouth act, he might even produce vials or tubes of blood from his pockets and blend these with yours right in front of you, acting as his own mixologist.

There is a very fine line between a vampire's high enjoyment of blood as blood, and his reaching a point where blood becomes an object of such intense interest and objectification that acting in this way removes the vampire from real engagement with everything else in his world—his coven, his culture, his physical world, and his woman.

This can happen because of traumas suffered in a vampire's earliest days, owing to his complete inexperience with the necessities of survival as a vampire and a very quick, brutal learning process. A vampire might also have gone through a period of starvation caused by a number of factors: imprisonment or isolation, human migration, or disasters. Starvation can badly affect a vampire's pleasure in blood, leading to occasional idolatry when memories of starvation overpower him. There can also be lingering affects of neuroses or mental disorders suffered during his human life, or hidden deficiencies of character that lead him to perverse behavior as a vampire.

If you think your vampire tends to acts of blood idolatry, and thus just wants you to fulfill his narrow-minded need, the main remedy is to discover the reason for the behavior. Try to find out what triggers his idolizing actions—what thoughts overcome him in the moments before he meets you? Ask him what he is thinking when he handles, studies, and drinks your blood in such a way as to separate you entirely from the act. More than likely, he will be filled with flashbacks to those moments when he had to overcome starvation as a very new vampire, in situations that he often mishandled. He might also be wracked by memories of a dead lover from years past, and take to blood itself as a symbol of that person.

The first remedy is to insist your vampire use no containers and drink directly from the bite or cut in your skin. As he does so, caress and massage him, and use other techniques—swinging motion, saunas—to reinforce the sensation of the blood flowing in him as an extension of you. Repeatedly create situations that reinforce physically his connection to you and that you are the source of his nourishment. A blood-idolizing vampire might breeze through or ignore sex, or lapse from the previous intensity of your sex life, so insist that his feeding lead directly to intercourse and continue during sex.

## Dealing with Your Vampire's Past

The first question to ask yourself about your vampire's past is, do you even really want to deal with it? There's nothing, really, that you can do about it, if there are elements or figures from one of his previous *centuries* that bug you. As long your blood-drinking boyfriend has no backward-looking hang-ups, or memories that cause problems in your relationship now, then you have little reason to make an issue of any part of his past.

But if he does have some sort of problem, it will relate to one of three things: a human lover he left behind; an early love of his vampire life; or a lost love from his vampire past. In each of these cases, your vampire might currently be drawn to women who remind him of a lost love. He might ask you to dress in certain ways that recall this person. You might realize that he wishes to act out events or roles that mimic his involvement with this woman.

Any attempt on his part to refocus his attention on someone other than you, even if she is long dead, might strike you as insulting and objectionable. In general, it certainly is, and your vampire will have to perform his remembrances of lovers past on his own, without bothering you about them. That's simply not fair, and you'll have to tell him so.

But you might also see this as an opportunity to exorcise something that has bothered him for a long time, and help him get it out of his system. Lost lovers tend to be idealized in the present, conscious mind, and thoughts of them can disallow a full expression of love in the present romance. So, though it might seem a subordination of yourself, a role-playing approach to solving your vampire's continued obsession with a lost lover might bring about some insight into those feelings that results in a complete transfer of affection to you, or clarity about the uselessness of those old feelings.

Don't get me wrong—you need not act like someone else to get your vampire to love you, or to love you more. But forcing someone to cram their feelings back inside themself is akin to driving vice underground: It still goes on, but in secret. Getting your lover to describe openly his feelings and act them out in some way gives him

Human lovers are not the only people whom vampires come to know and care about. I have, in the course of my life in the blood state, made both lasting and temporary human friends, all involved in the effort to maintain a peaceable buffer between the human and vampire world, and to develop useful alliances across that buffer. In my life, a Maryland farmer, a Virginia police detective, and, believe it or not, a delivery driver for a major shipping company all became close and crucial friends as I went about my endeavors and romances. With both the farmer and detective, there was the temptation to turn them into an actual situation in which to address pent up feelings of want. Additionally, I can assure you, that he will see clearly how you are trying to help him, for you are indeed helping him repair a part of his identity, and you will thus put your own stamp on him in doing so.

vampires, as I thought they would make strong members of my coven. But I knew they would refuse the join the blood state, and so I never broached the subject. And I mourned deeply both of them upon their deaths. They reminded me of the solid, upstanding men I knew as a boy in Massachusetts. So even in friendships and business associations, lives of the past that are now gone will occasionally give a vampire pause—this is simply a factor of having such long life. My delivery man, however, is quite alive and kicking at this time, and with no questions asked shipped out this evening an important package bound for an important recipient up north. Thank goodness for presigned labels.

But what of the vampire who refuses to confront his obsession over a lost love? He likes the whole brooding drama and hauntedness of it, eh? Well, there's only so much gothic emotion you can take before you will wonder exactly what you mean to him. If he's so caught up in the past, why does he have you in the present?

In such a situation, you're going to have to make the case for the heartening effects of you and your romance with him. They say that people who forget the past are doomed to repeat it. But vampires who agonize over the past are doomed to subjugate the present. So you might have to send him on his way.

## Human Hang-ups about and Objectification of Vampires

As you move along in your romance with your vampire, you will no doubt snag yourself on your own preformed ideas about these beings. You might also develop objectifying attitudes about them once you get to know a vampire. While such things might help form a defensive mental barrier against any interest in other vampires (and thus keep your mind from straying), any ill-formed notion will color and cloud your romance. This won't be helpful to the extensive communication you and your vampire lover need. So consider this brief list of the human prejudices I have met with in women, and see if you identify any in yourself. These are not egregious sins—just things that will hinder your perception and pleasure. You don't want that, do you?

1.  **VAMPIRES ARE INDESTRUCTIBLE:** Don't depend on it. Anything alive can be killed, and as I've said, vampires are very much alive, not "undead." Vampires are tough, but we can be physically destroyed. So don't fool yourself into thinking we're your own private Clark Kent who can take a bullet for you because we love you. We might indeed take that bullet, and we might survive, or we might not. The old methods—a wooden stake or metal shaft through the heart, or decapitation, or immolation—all work too damn well.

2.  **VAMPIRES ARE MURDERERS:** If we killed as many people as we fed from, we would first destroy our local food source and, secondly, bring upon ourselves a wave of vampire hunting and extermination. Yes, some violent or monstrous vampires

kill their victims, and there's been more than one serial killer who was also a vampire. But on the whole, the smart, gallant vampire who is simply trying to survive, maintain his cover, and assume his role in vampire society is not going to take more blood than humans can give safely, including, perhaps, a few black-outs and fainting spells among some of his "victims."

3. **VAMPIRES ARE INSATIABLE SEX MACHINES:** Satiation is, indeed, the real goal—enough food in the belly, and enough physical delight and love that one can feel *alive*. We tend to a longer, more vigorous performance, but an achievable, enjoyable climax is where we're headed, as are you. We're not machines.

4. **VAMPIRES HAVE NO SPIRITUAL LIFE, OR ARE IN LEAGUE WITH SATAN:** The orthodox person—Christian, Jewish, Muslim, Buddhist, etc.—is quite surprised and at a loss for words upon realizing he or she has been transformed into a creature that, living on blood, can live for millennia. It turns a lot of orthodoxy and religious belief on its head. I have known vampires who still believe in Jehovah, Allah, Moses, and Christ but have had to put their own beliefs through significant permutations to allow for their own existence. Other vampires recognize that what they have become is a

force of this Earth, and any fealty they owe belongs to the powers of this planet. Thus, they worship the natural world and that which is natural in vampires—the consumption of blood and the bond of blood (consider, as a corollary, the role of the Sacrament in contemporary Christian churches). As for Satan, well, I have always thought that *evil* is animal savagery in the service of reason and art. Only humankind possesses reason and art, so evil originates there, with *Homo sapiens* and the cerebral cortex.  No one I know has seen a devil.

5. **VAMPIRES SEEK TO CREATE HAREMS OF HUMAN WOMEN:** To be frank, some do, others don't. A vampire's first goal is securing a steady, nutritious, and highly accessible food source. If he does this by stringing together a network of willing or semiwilling women upon whom he feeds, and with whom he perhaps has sexual relations, then he is surely a rover and swordsman, though he might also be an otherwise peaceable fellow. If you, as your vampire's girlfriend, have had equal share in creating your relationship, and feel that you are a true and equal partner, then you in no way belong to a "harem," even if your vampire tends to feed mostly from other human women while loving none of them.

6. **VAMPIRES ALWAYS CONVERT THEIR VICTIMS AND LOVERS:**
No, not true. In fact, conversion usually backfires, because
the vampire will have posited in his own midst a creature
that will now compete with him for a limited food source. No
vampire makes that mistake. Conversion occurs in situations
of extreme need: during wartime, when new vampires are
needed to beef up covens or vampire forces; and when a
vampire so desires his human lover he wants her to enter into
a true blood marriage. There are those fanged chaos makers
out there who do convert too many victims, or select specific
victims, such as maniacs, and convert them, out of a perverse
and devilish pleasure. Your gallant fellow is not among these
wackos.

7. **VAMPIRES ARE ALL SECRETLY RICH, WITH HOARDS OF
MONEY AND JEWELS:** Older vampires who have survived for
over half a millennium surely have amassed some significant
material value. You'd be a foolish vampire if you didn't.
But you cannot assume that your vampire boyfriend has a
treasure trove somewhere. He will be well financed, surely—
enough to do those things he wishes to do. He can also
participate in financial systems created by covens. As said
earlier, you needn't worry about money while involved with
your vampire, as he will secure financing—he's used to doing

this, and money doesn't mean to vampires all that it means to humans, because there are few things a vampire can't steal. Paying for such things is simply good camouflaging practice. Is your vampire going to be your sugar daddy? Well, only if that's the kind of arrangement you seek and make clear that's how you want it, but the blood-to-sugar exchange rate is steep, my dear.

8. **VAMPIRES ARE DIRTY AND DISEASE RIDDEN:** Just like humans, and as an extension of their human practices of hygiene, your vampire's cleanliness is a case by case issue. We to tend to get a little dusty sometimes, especially if we have been traveling and sleeping out of doors, to say nothing of corralling and feeding from a horse, if times are lean. As for diseases, yes, we do carry some, as noted before. Our oral care is the biggest issue for you.

9. **YOU MUST ALWAYS HAVE A WEAPON ON HAND IN CASE YOUR VAMPIRE GETS OUT OF CONTROL:** Not unless he is starving will your vampire "get out of control," and then he'll only want to feed, not harm you. Possessing some sort of self-defense weapon, however, is a perfectly reasonable idea, as one of your vampire's greatest fears is that he might accidentally lead another, much more predatory vampire to you, one that is stalking him.

10. **YOUR VAMPIRE CAN HELP YOU GET AHEAD IN LIFE:** What shall he do—severely weaken all the other girls trying out for the cheerleading squad, and when it comes time for tryouts, you'll be the obvious star? In reality, a vampire can help you, to a degree, to secure those things you want in life. But you have to have the real talent to make the grade, and there's nothing he can do that will outrageously upset the invisible balance between the human and vampire worlds that keeps the mantle of camouflage over his head. For example, let's say you're working on an important report for your boss, and you would benefit greatly from being able to view a document that you can't get your hands on by usual means. OK, he'll bring you that document, if you ask. But he's not going to scare or hypnotize your boss into giving your report such high praise that you get an automatic promotion.

## Addressing a Possible Breakup

This might be the trickiest subject of all, more than blood, sex, or security. Human-vampire romances are subject to such strong dynamics that they have a high burnout rate. Then there's always the question of being in love with someone who is hardly aging.

Your romance will have its own factors that contribute to resolvable problems, or, perhaps, to a situation that can be resolved only by breaking up. Given the variety and particularity of such factors, I cannot address them all. But I can address their effects and consider the state of wanting to break up, or almost breaking up, and then consider the affects of an actual breakup. Such sorrows . . .

## When You Begin to Think It's Not Working

Women tend to have a better talent for putting a brave face on a relationship than men do. Behind that face, however, their instincts are almost always right. So when you begin to have the following concerns about your romance with your vampire, you might have to think seriously and decide on a course of action.

*He arrives on time and drinks my blood, but it feels like he's just going through the motions:* Every now and then, romance can become momentarily dull, through no one's fault. But if after a number of weeks of sheer repetitiveness, maybe you both just aren't as focused as you once were. Something might be awry, especially if the rituals of feeding seem perfunctory and the sex credible but bland.

*I don't care if he can't stay until near dawn anymore:* Perhaps some of the initial excitement has worn off your relationship, and you're being a bit more practical. But you might also be exhausted with the nocturnal nature of the romance, and would rather sleep.

***He was kinky at first, but now I'm a little weirded out:*** You probably can't describe your sexual limit the way you can read the wording of a law or safety rule, but you know it when you hit it too many times. So your vampire went from making love to you on a bearskin rug to asking you to wear a plushy, stuffed animal outfit? Too creepy for you?

***In my heart I know I can't sustain a secret relationship:*** The first five or six months of your vampire romance have gone fine, but with one hitch: It bugs you that you can't introduce many, if any, of your friends to your man. There's no doubt that a woman's significant other is a central figure in her social life. So you either use a stand-in, have a human boyfriend, or even a husband, and keep the back window open for your vampire on designated nights. But if you love him the most, and want a "human style" love in the sense that you can both cavort openly in social situations and your man sits down to eat your mother's blood pudding casserole on holidays, then this romance probably cannot last.

***I'm worried about the future, because we won't mature together:*** At some point, you will picture yourself and your vampire ten years from now. He is the same, and with all due kindness you will have to imagine yourself a decade older. How many more times are you willing to formulate that image in your head? Do you think that you can handle a long-term relationship in which only you age? Do you think he can? You might think that you can, but have doubts about him.

***We can't ever marry, because I won't marry into the vampire world:*** Your vampire might not want to be married, either. You can make it work as committed girlfriend and boyfriend for a long time. If marriage as a life stage is essential to you, however, then perhaps what you are doing now is simply a strange or alternative romance that you know will not last, yet will be interesting for as long as it can be. But, how long?

## When He Begins to Think It's Not Working

A vampire's hunger and amorous interest in you can appear to dominate his better judgment, but behind the fangs, we are most attuned to ourselves and to you. A vampire is something of a pleasure and happiness meter, being that those things are so crucial to him and of such clear frequency, given the otherwise demanding, even harsh nature of the vampire life.

So he's going to pay attention to his own senses and feelings about your romance. And he might begin to develop some questions of his own, which you won't be surprised to learn if you have to talk it out.

*I wonder why she's no longer so adventurous:* Long past are those weekend escapes to the mountains or lake districts, where the hunting was good, and you and your vampire could cavort as if you lived in another time. Now your meetings are bracketed by your schedule, for the usual reasons: work, sleep, social life. He's wondering if you're losing interest completely, or just trying to mold your romance into something more accommodating.

*She doesn't like our going out together in public anymore:* While venturing out to private or public venues is always risky, it is a pleasure for him to mill around in the human world with you. When you don't seem to enjoy that anymore, he's going to question if you are worried about being seen by your friends, or just want to keep the whole thing a secret. But behind the latter sentiment is the question of whether you want to continue the romance at all.

*She seems to enjoy less and less the feeding ritual, and is eager to have it over:* If your concerns about the relationship manifest themselves by a decrease in your enjoyment of his feeding on you, he will notice immediately, and continue to notice as long as your lack of enjoyment is detectable. If for some reason you've developed a dislike of him bleeding you and feeding this will be a major signifier to him.

*She isn't very concerned about setting specific dates to meet, or meeting in secure places:* The demands of secrecy and specific meeting times can be a bother when romance hinges on impulse and the impromptu. Though you might enjoy the excitement of being with your boyfriend, you might become tired of how bracketed your meetings can be sometimes, if for a period of time, his security and yours becomes a significant issue (as when another vampire might be pursuing you, or a vampire-hunting team is pursuing him).

***She won't wait if I can't get to her until a late hour:*** In the bloom of romance, you were willing to stay up all night for him. Now, if he can't make it by midnight, you're zonking out; you'll catch him over the weekend. Is this simply a sleep issue, or have you started to cool on the idea entirely?

## Right Idea, Wrong Vampire?

Perhaps what underlies your waning interest is that he's just not the right one. Of course, if he's your first one, how would you know if this is true romance? He might be gallant and good to you, but beyond that, there's no click of personalities. You were swept off your feet by the midnight excitement, but when all is said and done, you lack a connection.

This, more than anything, tells you that you simply have been involved with the wrong vampire. While he was fun, and a very good introduction, now that you know what enjoyments and excitements

**Do vampires cry?** I don't know how many women have asked me this question, and they clearly put a lot of stock in the answer. While we do not have the sheer abundance of tears that humans do, when deeply anguished or forlorn, we can and do indeed cry. But this is not the usual human weepiness over those pedestrian things you can't control—something must go really, *really* wrong to wring tears from a blood drinker. In my years as a vampire I have shed tears only in the wake of death, the truest end of all, and also on the day I left Violet behind. The conclusions of some of my romances have left me greatly bereft, dulled, and saddened, but my life went on and so did hers, and there is no crying over being alive. And, no, we do not cry *blood*. But our teardrops are tinged with pink.

you can have with a man of the night, you might have to move on to meeting one who is a closer match to you specifically.

But that is, indeed, a tall order, as you simply can't meet them on Craigslist, or is there now a "WSV" category? This is where meeting covenmates, and the girlfriends of covenmates, can be helpful, though that might sound calculated. But otherwise you're back to trial and error.

## Managing a Breakup

Breaking up with a vampire is a bit tricky. If your vampire is young (in both vampire and human years), a breakup will bring harsh frustration to him. But what will bother him more is to be deceived in this painful process, so, as with all other things, directness and clarity are necessary, even though you will want to soften the blow.

The first thing is to tell him your specific reason for leaving the relationship and how important this reason is to you. Most any reason is valid, as the human heart is a strange thing, but you can't fake this. In other words, if you find yourself attracted to another vampire, or a human, then be honest, rather than make use of a seemingly valid reason, such as your concern about your aging faster than him.

Your vampire will first want to know how seriously you hold this conviction. If you have truly concluded you do not love him, despite the effort you put into the experiment, or you have developed a serious attraction to someone else, then you must say so. Your vampire will most likely have a number of questions pertaining to things that he feared you disliked about him, the relationship, or vampirism in general. "Do you not like being bitten?" "Are you bothered by my feeding on others?" "Are you tiring of our romance being entirely nocturnal?" are the sorts of questions he will ask. You need to answer them directly and candidly, because he'll have a good sense of when you're not being wholly honest. Also, you'll make a clean break if you confirm that you aren't tired or repelled by the nature of a vampire-human relationship but have had a true change of heard about two individuals: you and him.

What if he doesn't take this well? That depends on the degree of his dislike. Most any vampire will be greatly saddened, even heartbroken, but we will have to accept your word and take it as the truth. If your vampire gets angry, and he might, he won't hurt you, though he might not hide his anger either, and an angry vampire is a sight to behold. If you feel threatened by this, he will leave if you ask him to leave. His code of honor doesn't evaporate at this bad news.

But the real question will be whether or not you let him taste your blood one last time. He might ask for this. If you refuse, then, truly, you have ended the relationship. Letting him taste your blood one last time, but withdrawing yourself or your wrist after a most brief drink is a somewhat more considerate approach.

Only a few vampires get rough about this, and this roughness was probably apparent early on in the relationship. A vampire might demand one last drink of your blood even if you refuse, and an uncouth fellow will force himself upon you to feed.

Would he also hurt you, in his anger over the breakup? A bad fellow might, just as any human could turn out to have a nasty side when things, in his view, go wrong. More than likely, however, a vampire, no matter how agitated and saddened by your decision, will cause no actual harm because he wishes none to come to you.

## When the Vampire Ends the Romance

There will be those relationships in which the vampire is the one to end it, whether the woman sees it coming or not. Every vampire knows he could just disappear and never see his now ex-girlfriend ever again, but that is hardly in keeping with being the good sort who attracted her in the first place.

Why might a vampire break up with you? He might do so because he has met another woman, someone who perhaps connects him psychologically to something crucial in his past; or someone who is more amenable to the way he lives his life (my rambling and roving come to mind); or someone to whom he is so attracted he wishes to take her as a blood bride (especially if he knows you would not go this far). He might also end your romance because he must move away from the place where you are, due to a major safety issue, or because of a duty to his coven. Lastly, he might decide that in fact a vampire romance is wrong for you or your life, no matter what you have told him; he might peer into the future and see your romantic presence as an evolving liability.

There is always the possibility, too, that his initial attraction has faded. If in your case you successfully sought this vampire, as opposed to him finding you, he might have entertained the romance for a while, but ultimately "deselected" himself when he realized that he wasn't as attracted to you as you were to him.

How will he break up with you? He will most likely try to do it in one single moment. He will arrive when he says he will arrive, but he will not drink your blood. He will, instead, tell you the thing that you don't want to hear. He will explain as clearly as he can, though he won't tell you who he is leaving you for, if that is the case, or where he is going, if he has to go away. But he will be willing to create a way that you can get a message to him after the breakup, because he will still want to be able to keep in touch if something serious comes up—something to do with your safety.

If you have an argument against a breakup, he'll listen. But dissuading a vampire on this subject is difficult if he has made up his mind. To make his decision, he will consider the long view of your life and his, which isn't entirely different from the way humans make judgments about their romances (and such judgments, harsh as they might seem, must be made). He will be considering seriously the impact his life could have on yours, and what that could mean in relation to your much shorter longevity.

Don't feel unfairly judged by your human mortality. Every day is a small judgment in mortality, for both humans and vampires, because the sand is running out—faster for you than for me. This makes decisions about your life all the more crucial and time sensitive.

This is not a cut-and-dry vampire assessment any more than a human male's decision to break up with a woman is simple. But the act of breaking up itself is never anything to be drawn out. The actual break should be a quick thing, really. Who wants to belabor that, riding it around like a horse?

## After the Romance Ends

The end of a romance is a depressing time, no matter how you look at it. It often feels like a failure at life itself, given that being happy is usually our biggest goal; even us blood drinkers endeavor toward a kind of happiness, albeit with a largely different standard.

Most women who've broken up with a vampire say the first thing that overcomes them is sleep. This is obviously a combination of being down emotionally and no longer having to dedicate a

chunk of your life to night hours. After that comes a strong sense of something inexplicable. Your relationship with your vampire will seem like an enigma because it had so many out of the ordinary and seemingly fantastic elements. Many women, post vampire, speak of a strange feeling of displacement, as if they've been in an alternate reality, and they experience a mild to strong culture shock as they return to a regular, all human life.

Some women attempt to seek out their former lover, if not to convince him to return, then at least to see him again for the sake of finding out how he is and if he is well. The chances of physically locating him by chance are remote. As you've probably learned by this point in your experience with such creatures, if a vampire does not want to be found, he won't be found.

But, as stated above, your vampire, in the process of becoming your ex-lover, will present a way for you to stay in contact. Most likely, this will be a way to post actual, physical messages to each other, or communicate through coded graffiti. You won't be able to carry on a continual conversation this way, like the rapid back and forth of any of the compulsive digital communications, but the important information will get through.

## Another Vampire?

The postbreakup time will be the truest test of your possessing, or not possessing, a true liking for vampires. For now that you now what it is like to lose one, you can make a full evaluation of your interest in these nighttime paramours: You will know if you want to give vampires another go, or if vampiric relationships are simply unsustainable to you, given that the vampire will be the one who leaves you, sooner or later or much later.

But if after your initial romance, you know for sure that you prefer a vampire over a human man, then you will set off again in search of another. This time, the endeavor will be easier. You will probably have an idea of the haunts of your ex-boyfriend's coven-mates, and of the habits of local vampires in general. You know how to endure blood loss and enjoy the feeding process. The initial encounter with a new vampire will not be a total surprise, but it will have pleasurable familiarities.

You will also know something else: how attracted you are to vampirism in general, and how interested you might now be in making the ultimate conversion, from human to vampire. That is what might have been lurking underneath your romantic interest all along. Once you know this, encountering another vampire is not just a romantic desire—it is a passionate goal.

But conversion is not something to pursue halfheartedly. You are talking about leaving behind nearly every human connection in your life, and most everything human in yourself. This is the metaphorical death of transformation, and it is nearly as thorough as actual, physical death itself, hence the hoary old expression "undead." Do not give up your human life and human self unless you possess the most profound realization that your existence as a human is nil.

This is an extraordinary situation, but it is also inherent to the vampire romance. So turn please to the next, and final, chapter.

# 8

# The Ultimate Acts: Marrying a Vampire and Conversion

What if your vampire romance turns out great? This fellow has become the love of your life, and despite the differences in your physiology, personal history, social lives, and diet, you have a connection that makes more amorous sense than anything you've ever known. You might suddenly think that this thing has the potential for serious commitment. You as a human can marry a vampire—you don't have to *be* a vampire to marry one.

But commitment won't happen overnight. You and your boyfriend will need to rack up a significant amount of time together, and overcome some obstacles, before anybody starts talking about a more permanent connection. More than anything, you'll have to consider the implications for your family—unless you're mostly on your own—and for your career. Society isn't kind to the woman who does not (apparently) marry, and who continues in singlehood into her middle and later years.

But let's consider the what-ifs of taking the plunge with a vampire. I base these views entirely on the longest committed relationship of my vampire years, and also what I have witnessed of other human-vampire connections that moved into commitment and marriage.

Beyond that, this last chapter will consider the final act of your vampire connection: your conversion into the blood state. This in and of itself is probably another book entirely, but because this can be the result of your vampire relationship (and also possibly its end) I will detail it at some length. It is, to some minds, a highly amorous, most desirous fantasy in the making.

## Would You Marry Your Vampire?

On its face, marriage among vampires or with a vampire seems unnecessary. In the blood state there is the ability to act with minimal restriction, and while many vampires are committed to their coven-mates or other vampires, the kind of romantic fidelity that marriage requires appears on its surface to be unsuited to my kind.

But remember that there is still something in us that is somewhat human, or a throwback to our humanity. We still love and desire love. And if the woman we love has both the serious want and need for a formal commitment, there are those of my fanged brethren who will make that commitment with her. The question I must pose and attempt to answer here is why *you* would want to marry your vampire boyfriend (let's assume he is or will be open to the idea).

A first significant reason, far beyond any compatibility test, is that you derive from this romance an indescribable fulfillment. This might be better described as something "spiritual" between you and your vampire. Such fulfillment can derive from a combination of the intensity of your emotional and sexual bonds and your feeling of being protected.

Secondly, you will realize that you might not ever again have so meaningful a connection with a being so powerful as this one. Given your willingness to act outside the usual human social order—or, at the very least, to live a life of no outwardly visible means of support—a vampire can provide a great deal for you. Imagine being able to do whatever it is you've always wanted to do. As long as what you want to do actually means something; anybody can loaf by the swimming pool and shop, and doing so for days on end will not impress a vampire.

From 1885 to 1910, I remained with the same woman, Jocelyn, and I considered this a blood marriage. We performed the ceremony unto ourselves, with no witnesses, thus not making it official in any sense except to ourselves. We lived just south of Charleston, South Carolina. She was the widow of a respected Confederate veteran, and as such was given a good deal of leeway and respect socially. She had been married off at the age of fifteen, something she resented but agreed to nonetheless. She was twenty-eight when I met her. I was roving the South as an observer—indeed, as a spy, for my coven—and I found myself enchanted by her, first because she showed no fear of me at all and laughingly told me that she expected more from the "boogeyman." She lived on the plantation bequeathed her by her husband's family, and I was able to dwell there under very good cover, both for her sake

Lastly, you will understand that this longing you have contained for so long, an inexplicable desire for something not clearly known that has been fulfilled by your love for your vampire, has also brought its concomitant epiphany: Your life as a human woman is and mine, while my business took me into Charleston, Savannah, and Atlanta. But soon enough I was in love with her, and she told me that I opened a sexual world she had not yet known, only imagined, and also liberated her from the expectations of family and her many suitors. While I was sometimes gone for weeks, even months at a time, I always found my way back over the Savannah River to her. She didn't remind me of any woman I had known in my human life, but seemed to me to be the woman I should have always met had I remained a man (remember, as a human I married young—happily so, but young). Only when she came to the difficult but right decision that she wanted, and needed, a human husband for her later years did she and I mutually decide that I should move on. She died in 1930. I put flowers on her grave every March 21, the day we met.

meant for this union and did not fit any role in society as you knew it. In other words, you have awoken to a destiny.

If you know in your heart all three of these things about your vampire love—a spiritual bond, openness to its potency, and a personal sense of destiny—you have grounds for matrimony. But unlike human marriage, matrimony with a vampire cannot be undone while both partners are living. Once that complete bond of blood is made, you will always have a vampire husband. It will not be any sort of usual marriage, though it uses human nuptials as a model. It will be flexible, to accommodate both human and vampire necessities. The life of its human partner determines its duration.

## The Nature of the Vampire Wedding

A vampire wedding ceremony is usually a simple but poetic act carried out in the same manner, whether the marriage is between a human and vampire, or two vampires. The bride and groom wear special vestments, usually silk robes over lighter garments; these vestments will be stained with the blood of the couple and kept so as to be worn at special anniversaries, or when the couple themselves attend a vampire wedding.

The wedding will take place in a common area in a coven. If the wedding is that of a vampire and a human female, the vampire drinks blood from a number of spots on the woman's body—the wrist, neck, and breast—while the bride makes a cut in the groom's wrist, and swirls a few droplets of his blood into a glass of water, wine, or tea, and drinks that (as said earlier, drinking a small amount of diluted vampire blood does not induce conversion).

Marrying vampires will drink each other's blood directly from each other's bodies in several places.

The chief of a coven might serve as a kind of official, but more crucial are the vampire witnesses who observe the vampire feed upon his bride, the human bride taste a small quantity of her groom's blood, and their blood stain each other's vestments. The witnesses also hear the bride and groom exchange their vows, which contain several traditional lines that your vampire can reveal the night before the wedding only. These vampires will then mark in the coven's record their witnessing the marriage, and your establishment as "wife and husband of the blood state." No, you won't need a license; a blood test is pointless.

Your groom will most likely choose a fellow called his "second." This expression goes back to the days of duels. In the case of a coven, the second is the vampire who must go instead if some duty calls upon the groom, allowing the marriage to proceed. It is a position of honor, but rarely is the second called away on a mission meant for the groom.

As the bride, you can bring a human witness—someone of maximum trustworthiness, most likely the person who was in the know during your vampire romance—but the usual train of bridesmaids will not be possible. This also leaves out family, unless your witness is a relation.

The chief of the coven, the second, and any honored guests will most likely taste your blood, either drawn into a chalice, or with a brief kiss to a cut on the wrist. As I said, this will only be a taste; you will not be feasted upon. But a feast will have been prepared, to be sure, either in the form of willing humans (recall the earlier discussion of the blood brothel), hypnotized humans, or quality livestock, if possible. For you, the bride, there will be your favorite foods, and there will be cake: half angel food and real icing, half jellied blood, with blood-paste icing and blood candies, and other vampiric confections.

Dancing, music, toasts, songs, and games will last all night. Then you and your new husband will take to a secret sleeping place, possibly within the coven structure, or not far from it. Traditionally, for the first full cycle of the moon that you are married, you will be expected to live by your vampire's hours: sunset to sunrise. Some couples truncate this to a week, given the human job market. But there has lately been a turn back to a more formal nuptial initiation.

# Living as Wife and Vampire Husband

I once had a woman tell me that she had a reoccurring dream when she was with me: She was on vacation in Hawaii, or somewhere like it, and she went out on the beach at night. She could see another island nearby, and she heard me call her from there. But she had to swim through very dark water to get to me. She was scared, but she went, and met me on the black sand, knowing she could never swim back.

"But," I told her, "we had a whole entire Hawaiian island to ourselves." That seemed like a pretty good turn of events to me. I'm not sure, however, if she felt the same way. Indeed, we did not marry.

In some ways, that woman's dream raises the biggest issue facing the intermarriage of human and vampire: that you are on something of an island, unto yourselves, in the sea of humanity. Humans outnumber vampires something like "one million:one" in this world. How you cope in that world, in the long run, as a dedicated couple is something you will have to figure out before getting married.

The thing is, a vampire can't change his being a vampire. No one has ever discovered a reversal of the conversion; believe me, the experiments continue, for the sake of figuring out exactly what vampirism is—operating on the theory that if you can reverse a process, you understand the whole system. So, the person who might make a major life change is you, the woman. Please don't feel put upon by this. I've addressed this earlier in this section; you wouldn't be taking this plunge if this change isn't what you sought.

You can continue with your human social life, your career, even motherhood and childrearing while married to your nocturnal one. In some cases, you will have to. And in some cases, women in such situations have also carried on with their human husbands, who knew little to nothing about the vampiric side of their wives' lives, but that is indeed an extraordinary situation, and one that is probably impossible in the digital age.

You can refer to this as a "double life," if you wish. But it is really a life within a life. Whatever is your outward, public, "daylight life," as my kind call it, you will have that very private space that only you and your vampire occupy. You will realize a kind of perfection in yourself for becoming capable of this balance.

Then there are those women who completely turn themselves over to a vampirelike existence, living mostly a nocturne, going where their vampire goes, having abandoned most habitual human contact except for a few most trusted friends or relations. More women do this than you might expect. But it is a tough life, and if you choose this, you will not be able to follow your husband everywhere if he is part of a coven and has occasional duties to that group.

Some couples work out a period of rambling and adventure, and then choose a very good location in which to settle down, one that allows the wife to create (or recreate) a somewhat regular life, with job, friends, children, and, if necessary, a human spouse. Her vampire husband will always be close, and they will continue to maintain their romance, this life within a life.

And yet there will be all those things that make up the simple details of married life—budgets, laundry, home furnishings, insurance—that will make this seems as typical as any human marriage. These things are inescapable, because you have to save and spend wisely, you have to have a place to sit, you have to have clean clothes, and you have to be able to pay for the occasional rainy day. There will be that moment in the grocery store when you finish ticking off your list, and you realize that you never have to cook for him, and how strange that is, although he will teach you how to prepare various blood-based treats.

Now, to put to rest that old idea of vampire polygamy: Those of us blood-drinking fellows who enjoy the company of human women, and then enjoy one woman so much that we commit to her, do so with just her. A blood marriage is a one-at-a-time thing,

While I might sound as if I have over the years created my own circus of women, I did so romance by romance. I am for the most part a serial monogamist when it comes to you mortal ladies, and while that term "serial" might have some unpleasant implications for a human boyfriend (he just won't commit, will he?) for the vampire it is simply a facet of our extreme longevity. But I have in my years encountered several male vampires who had strung together such amazing networks of females, both human and vampire, as to earn their status as the Don Juans, Errol Flynns, and Tom Joneses of North American vampirism. The oldest vampire I know in North America, a fellow of Seminole descent who became a vampire in the early 1500s, claims to have had over five thousand human women lovers in his life, having lost count in the late 1800s. Another fellow, a member of an allied coven, who was converted in Naples in 1620, claims that at this very moment he has two human girlfriends in every state in the union, and has romantically attended over two thousand European and American women. Finally, my good friend Slyvka, a Ukrainian vampire now in the United States, who became a vampire shortly after World War I, says that only his discerning eye has limited him to just one hundred girlfriends, each of whom he says he truly loved, and five of which he married. And me—a "life list"? I'm too modest.

please. As I described earlier, there have been numerous vampires who cultivated a network of human female lovers, doing so for the creation of a flexible and diversified range of sustenance. The idea of making any one of them a wife would not have made sense, even to the vampiric libido, as there would be no point in becoming so dedicated to one when the group as a whole is what matters, each one getting attention in turn. Some male vampires continue this practice, and the idea of marriage is remote to them. But they do have that ability, similar to human men, to really, *really* like every single one of the women with whom they consort; they simply cannot settle upon one and only one.

# Seeking Conversion to Vampirism

You must be candid with yourself about the strong possibility that your amorous interest in vampires is your conscious expression of a deeply held want—that of becoming a vampire yourself. Thousands of humans, men and women, desire this, for any number of reasons: escape from an untenable personal or legal situation; sheer survival; fear of impending death; a want for vampiric power; a desire for an extremely long life.

For women who seek the blood state, I think there is also a political component, for becoming a vampire utterly liberates a woman from any typical female human role, and sets her on equal footing with male vampires. There might be a lot of swagger among the male contingent of the vampire world, but we are well aware that females of any kind no longer need us to reproduce, and also understand most clearly that female vampires could as roundly stomp us, confound us, and outmaneuver us as we could them.

If you sense this desire within yourself, you will have to address it before you embark upon a romance with a vampire, because you need to know if you will be too tempted to be converted by your vampire boyfriend who should know better and resist converting you at all, if ever. You should also understand if this is your whole motivation for a romance, because then this amorous connection is simply a means to an end, and you might not be able to just use a vampire in that way.

## The Temptations of Vampiric Power

There are ways to assess whether or not you are as much or more focused on becoming a vampire yourself than having a romance with a vampire. This is not an exact science, as we are dealing with a mostly unresearched frontier of the human mind—the want to be a vampire—but given what I've seen of women who wanted me and a few who wanted me for what I could do to them, the following are workable psychological criteria:

***Did an obsession with vampires begin in childhood?*** A romantic fascination with vampires as a young or adult woman is one thing. A long held, visceral interest that began way before sexual maturation is a different story. You have an interest in the vampiric that is integrated with your sense of identity. Using your vampire lover to turn yourself into a vampire is a fulfillment of your projected identity.

***Do you want to accompany your vampire on his adventures very soon after meeting him, no matter how impulsive this is or the costs to your life?*** If you happen to be this way because you can't get enough of the vampire himself, then you've simply become overly enamored of this fellow and are developing a deep attachment too rapidly. But if you are much more interested in the *how*, the *what*, the *where* of his rambling and duties, then it is the vampire life that draws you so deeply.

***Do you dream about being a vampire, even when not involved with one?*** Dreams are highly metaphorical and not up for easy interpretation, Freud notwithstanding. But if in your dreams of living in the blood state you see yourself doing very specific things, particularly things you never thought of before, and you find these dreams highly arousing and exciting, you probably harbor a lot of latent desire for vampirism.

***Do you encourage your vampire to feed heavily upon you?*** This is a displacement of desire, because when you do this, you imagine that you are in fact the vampire who is having herself a very nice, full drink. Also, you push yourself to derive a pleasure from the feel of his mouth and the wooziness of blood loss as a way of allowing yourself an empathy with future victims, as well as a rationale for thinking that victims can take pleasure in you having your dinner.

*Do you have a conscious list of goals in the blood state?* This can readily derive from your dreams of vampirism, and turn into a plan for adventure, one that you might even begin to review frequently as you go about finding your way to conversion into the blood state.

People who have these psychological symptoms have one other thing in common: a feeling of powerlessness in the human world that they believe will be most enjoyable to overcome in the form of a vampire. This powerless feeling begins at a young age, and usually coincides with the childhood obsession with vampires. The epic existence, physical and implied sexual powers, outlaw role, and opportunities at enrichment of the vampire become desirable beyond all other things to the mind of this person. These intense desires become layered in this person's character, to be acted upon later in life.

Now, what about the double whammy: As a child, you became obsessed with the identity and power of the vampire, and as an adolescent girl, your budding sexual identity created out of your preexisting interest a deep desire for vampires—so that now as an adult involved with a vampire, you're nuts about him, but you want him to convert you, too? From a purely individualized point of view, that's about as strong a come-on as you can find among the human crowd. Any vampire would be hard pressed not to fall right into a kind of romance about his own existence, created by your delighting in it and him.  But from a more collective view of the blood state, a vampire will have to keep his head and make a very selective decision about you, no matter how enthusiastic you are. A willing convert will be saddened and insulted that a vampire will make her his lover or wife but not convert her. This is a judgment that goes beyond you.

## Will Your Vampire Want to Convert You?

In the throes of making love to you and drinking your blood, every vampire will seriously consider converting his girlfriend, but this is an effect of passion, not logic. When we are most enjoying you— during our adventures, our exercises, our strange thrills—is when you will seem most right to join us in the blood state. Conversion tempts us vampires with the same kind of thrill that comes to the human mind with the thought of extending your line, genetics, name, and likeness. And then there is the fact that by draining you to unconsciousness, a wildly sensuous act of gluttony, and filling you up steadily with our own blood, we will preserve you as you are now, as lovely as you make yourself for your vampire, in the bloom of love or youth or both.

## Conversion Count

In my entire life in the blood state, I have converted a total of five people, two of whom were girl-friends. One of them asked me, after she thought about it for a long time, and once she became a vampire she remained my lover for a long time before I told her she would never be complete if she remained with me. So she took off on the necessary century-long adventure. She lives in France now, and is widely admired. With the other woman, I suggested conversion to her; although our romance was starting to wane after several years, I told her she was among few girlfriends who struck me as someone who would make a champion vampire. She agreed. She is now a key vampire historian in North America. Her archivist job in D.C. trained her well.

Under most circumstances, the last Factor of Blood applies, as stated in chapter 1. So, aside from the sheer libidinal want to convert you because you're do damned lovely and fun, these are the reasons or circumstances for conversion:

***Loss of a coven or significant coven members:*** Survivors of a fight between covens, the work of vampire hunters, or a vampire who disappeared during field work will try to reestablish what they once had. Continuity of vampire history and teachings is a major reason. Select human beings will be sought for rebuilding, and those already known as willing converts will be quickly found.

***A need to build up a coven, or create vampire soldiers:*** In times of great conflict, human or vampire, covens and vampire groups will be involved in varying degrees of warfare, and will need "conscripts," of a kind. This is the most unscrupulous of conversions, and is the way in which I became a vampire.

***A vampire who seeks a vampire spouse:*** Some vampires might carry on with human lovers but in the end will want a spouse who is fully informed about the blood state. A current human girlfriend might very well fit this bill.

***A human with whom a vampire is in love:*** Yes, our favorite subject. If you are game; if he thinks the blood state is right for you; if you both are well aware that being vampires might change your relationship entirely; and if you know you have long felt this calling, then . . . yes, it could happen. But be advised that your lover will have to think very highly of you as potential vampire material, something that can be mutually exclusive to his thinking that you are a very fine and lovely human being whom he adores.

## The Human and Moral Issues of Conversion

If you're remotely religious, you're going to have to adapt your beliefs in the face of vampiric conversion. As Shakespeare said, "There are more things in Heaven and Earth . . . than are dreamt of in your philosophy." I've always taken that as possibly the best suggestion for the religious person who is also deeply drawn to vampirism and possible conversion. It doesn't say, "Your religion is wrong"—it simply says there's more to this existence than you might have previously addressed.

In fact, the more fantastic things of which religions speak— virgin births, deaths and resurrections, cherubim, dragons—would seem even more possible given the nearly incredible fact of the existence of my kind. And while I did say that we vampires know nothing more of deities or devils than you know or don't know, i.e., we are not a league of or in league with ol' Scratch himself, there is the possibility that we and you humans are all part of a much larger cosmic order about which we make slow discoveries, piece by piece.

So the greater implications for you when it comes to turning into a vampire are your personal and professional responsibilities.

I once knew a doctor who wanted me to convert him so he could spend centuries helping humans with their health, but I refused on the grounds that his job at the hospital where he worked was too important. We compromised, and I waited until he retired, and now he practices medicine at night only.

But you will have to decide to leave behind entirely most of your human life and those people in it. Attempting to pass as a person with a rare skin disorder who cannot venture out in daylight won't work—it has been tried too many times and has too many pitfalls. So you must ask yourself how important you are to the people in your life: family members, friends, and members of your profession. If just one human life depends upon yours, your voluntary departure into the blood state will be tainted with that abdication.

You must also consider the contribution you will make to humanity across your lifetime. You're probably not doing your best work right now—that will come only in middle age, even your later years, when you can combine intelligence with experience and the long view so crucial to leadership. As a being who so greatly depends upon humans, in this utterly lopsided symbiosis you and I have, your future impact on the quality of life in the human world might far outweigh the pleasures you might have as a vampire.

Lastly, consider this: You might be a much better human being than a vampire. In other words, you might turn out to be a complete screwup once the fangs grow in.

Vampirism is a taxing state and a tough profession. If you're not ready for it, you might fail, and failure is death in my world. You don't want to know our mortality rates.

## Is Conversion the End of the Relationship?

As I've suggested before, some vampires have converted their human girlfriends and they lived together happily ever after for several centuries. I've also seen my share of heartbroken fellows who, upon teaching his newborn vampire girl how to hunt, realized he had a wild-eyed, overexcited lynx on his hands who promptly announced, "I'm *outta* here!" and disappeared into the night. Such is the thrill of feeling what's it's like to become a vampire.

The rest of us fall somewhere in the middle. No male vampire is foolish enough to think that conversion will result in perfection, or not put notions in his woman's head. And you, my reader, have no idea how you'll react once you are converted to the blood state. You might think you know, enthusiastic as you are, but you don't know, believe me. Imagine the sensation of being able to breathe underwater and fly like a bird all at the same time, while consumed by a relentless, mind-bending hunger. Sound like fun?

# Conversion: How It Happens

After having cut all unessential ties to your human life, your vampire will take you to a new location, one that can be kept very secure for a week or more. You will take with you some clothing and other essential personal items. Pack lightly. Your other belongings can be collected later. Ditch your cell phone, please (forget about the contract).

Eat your last meal no less than forty-eight hours before conversion. Yes, indeed, your last meal, and eat well—you'll need the nutrients. But then you must fast for two days.

It starts like this:

Your vampire will make a deep incision or bite in your neck, and will then feed from you heavily but in short sessions, stopping the flow of blood between. He should know his own system well enough, and know you well enough, that he will have an accurate idea of when he has imbibed nearly a third of your blood.

This is a lot of blood for you to lose. Along the way you will get groggy. You will get a headache. You'll get cold. And then you'll pass out. So in the later stage of feeding, you will be in bed, under blankets. Your blood pressure will be falling, and your body will try to compensate for this. Your vampire will carefully draw out this process of imbibing so you don't lose a lot of blood very quickly. When he is done, he will then fully seal the incision or bite mark, possibly with stitches so that there is no further blood loss.

The second stage is tricky. If you have lost consciousness, then your boyfriend will have to transfuse his blood directly into your body. He will know how to do this. In fact, it's probably the best way, because even though you're awake and could drink his blood, you want your blood pressure and volume to return to normal as quickly as possible, and a transfusion can make this happen more quickly.

Once your blood volume comes back to normal with vampire blood, you will very quickly begin to feel ill, very much like a rapid onset of influenza. You will ache, get chills, and feel feverish. Your boyfriend will do what he can to ease you through this. If you're given to panic attacks, you'll probably have a touch of that. But soon enough you will fall into an uncomfortable sleep. If you remember any dreams, they will be memories of a chaos of colors and light.

The vampire blood will go about its work, carrying the genetic material necessary to unwrap and rewrap the DNA of every cell in your body. Your body will literally swap human for vampire at the molecular level.

Over the four or five days necessary for a complete transformation, you will awaken numerous times, like a child in a fever. You might hallucinate. You might try to get out of bed. Your vampire will not leave your side during this time and will sleep with you, holding you when you flail and listening when you try to speak. The chamber will be lightproof, in case he must tend to you during daylight hours.

Before you awaken, your vampire must find your first meal, so he must leave you alone for a while. If you wake up alone, do not panic, but you will feel as if in a fever, and suffer from a thirst that is akin to starvation. He will return soon, with a victim he has taken into his control, and you will have your first taste of the blood that is life.

You will not be able to drink much. You will have to take sips and small mouthfuls. You will get used to the way your new body feels, with its weird sensations of energy and nimbleness; you will soon enjoy your ability to smell things keenly, and see through the night.

Before he teaches you to hunt, your fellow vampire will want to make love to you, feeding you heavily before you do, so that you may being to learn the great pleasures of blood, and how it feels inside you, how it feeds you, and how your physical enjoyment only heightens the inner sensation of being alive. What will become of you two as lovers cannot be known to either one of you, but before you can survive on your own, you will both enjoy again the intense, private pleasures you learned together months or years ago. But this time you will taste each other's blood and be forever locked in the blood state as vampires.